THE JOURNAL OF BRIAN DOYLE

A GREENHORN ON AN ALASKAN WHALING SHIP

BY JIM MURPHY

Scholastic Inc. New York

THE Florence
1874

May 4, 1874

Am belowdecks of the *Florence* now and safe. There are eighteen others with me in this gloomy wedge-shaped space, which is lined top to bottom with bunks and lit by a tin oil lamp that smokes. Another new man — we are called greenies — paced off the room and found it to be fourteen feet long by twelve at its widest.

That is eight cubits by seven cubits, announced another greenhorn named Nathaniel Burt. Had a strange smile on his face when he informed us that that was how Noah's ark was measured in Scriptures. Nathaniel's mention of Scriptures earned him several unkind remarks from those assembled.

Saw an empty bunk and sat in it. It was the lowest of three and not very big, but I thought I could make myself comfortable there. Settled back, but then a large man leaned over, grabbed my shirt, and hauled me out, ramming my head on the wood frame of the bunk above.

That put a scare in me the way Pa's rages could, not to mention a knot on my head. A man with a Scots accent named Watty Turnball said the big man's name is York — because he is from York, Pennsylvania — and that is his usual greeting.

My new bunk is at the very front where the ship and this room come to a point. Jim Browning — who is the oldest on the ship at thirty-eight and a greenie also — said the space made a "cozy little bunkhouse" and an annoyed voice called out, "This's the fur'castle, ya —" and finished his sentence with an impressive string of cusses. Nothing is said on a whaler, I have learned, without adding a colorful cuss or two. Resolved then to say as little out loud as possible. My reckless tongue got me in enough trouble at home.

We are anchored, but the ship still rolls and bobs in a way that sets my stomach in motion. Or maybe that is just the stink in here — of rotting fish, rancid whale oil, sweating, unwashed shipmates, tar and grease, piss, paint, and tobacco smoke.

But I don't care. I am away from him and when we leave San Francisco town tomorrow a.m. he won't be able to get at me.

York has ordered all greenies to shut up and go to sleep. Think he wants a quiet room so he and his pals can play cards in peace.

It is dead quiet in here. Except for York and his mates cussing their wretched luck, the occasional squeal of a pig on deck, and the sound of someone pacing just above us. So I am in my new home with my new family. And tomorrow, I, Brian Doyle, begin my new life as a whale hunter.

May 5

Can barely hold this pencil, my hands are so raw from hauling on hard ropes and climbing the rigging. Head is spinning dizzy from my bump and my stomach is restless besides. Thought I might write about my first full day aboard the *Florence*, but just now I can think of nothing but sleep. And my older brother, Sean Michael. But I don't think Pa will hurt him now that I'm gone.

Sometime later

Stomach and head not much better, but think writing might distract me. A mate of York — a black man from Brazil named Frenchie with a batch of wriggling snakes tattooed on his left arm — saw me writing and suggested I could write letters for him during the voyage. Thought it wise to say yes.

About my day. Woke to the sound of a bell clanging and shouts to look lively. I rolled out of my bunk and scrambled on deck with the others. No breakfast was served and since I slept in my clothes, all I had to do was slip on my shoes and not smash my head on the hatch.

On deck, a very angry-looking third mate — Mr. Green — was waiting to greet us with shouts and cusses. The moment he saw me he pointed skyward and screamed something about "settin' loose the foretops'l." When I hesitated, he went to slap my head, only I ducked, just as I do when Pa swings.

He let out a string of cusses about my "hangin' back" and took a step toward me, but I did not "hang back" to see what he had in mind. Had noticed York and Frenchie climbing up a rope ladder, so quick as a monkey I followed them up as well as I could.

And up they went, to where the lower sails of the forward mast were tightly furled. When York saw me his face colored red so fast I thought he might try to hit me, too, so I said, "Mr. Green said I was with you." This in no way pleased York, but at least the lie stayed his punch.

He told me I better listen sharp whenever he says something. Then he pointed out along the yardarm and gave me an order I did not understand any better than the one given by Mr. Green. Fortunately, Frenchie was there to explain what to do.

Dropped my legs around the yardarm and began pulling myself toward the outmost edge as quickly as I could. Which wasn't very quick! Glanced down once — a mistake! — and froze in place.

I've been on the roof of our house many times, but this was different. Only a thin arm of shaky wood was between me and crashing to the deck below. Frenchie shouted don't look down and to keep going, which I managed to do. Slowly.

The ship was alive with noise — of orders being shouted, of the windlass groaning as it hauled up the anchor, of the grunts and cusses of men. Add to that the squealing of six pigs, the bleating of two milk goats, and the jabber of three dozen or so chickens. Still, I could hear York mutter something unkind about "that clumsy mick" to Frenchie and Frenchie's reply that "the boy moves good up here for a greenie, York. Let'm be."

I fumbled some with my knot, but we had the big sail loose before any of the other sails on the *Florence* were adrift. Frenchie sang out, "All gone, the foretops'l," and Mr. Green replied, "Loose the to-gants'l and stays'ls." And up we bounded — at least I tried to bound — to our next task. We were leaving port with the *Thomas John*, which is owned by the same whaling company that owns the *Florence*. The *Thomas John* has a steam engine in addition to sails and Mr. Green wanted to beat her —

yes, the *Thomas John* is also referred to as a she!?! — to open sea.

More sails unfolded and filled up with the morning breeze. Then as the ship slowly turned to gather in more wind, all sails on the three masts snapped alive and the ship lurched forward, nearly shaking me from my perch. Soon, we were moving quite lively and leaving the wharf and San Francisco town behind.

That was when I noticed that the gentle movement of the ship had become less gentle. The mast was now waving back and forth and I was, too! Glanced at the water and discovered that every little wave was topped by winking flashes of light, each painful to the eyes. Cast my glance on the deck, but the ship's motion had set it moving this way and that, while men and animals went that way and this.

Closed my eyes, but this did not help, either. Felt every wiggle and every twitch of the ship, heard every shout. My mouth suddenly began to water and my stomach leaped about. "Puke," York screamed, "and I'll make you eat it!"

We had not even gone one thousand feet, had not even left the harbor. What would the open sea be like?

York did not let me worry long on this, ordering me down the ratlines — which is the name of the ropes used in climbing. We did not go down to rest or have breakfast. As soon as we hit wood we had new orders shouted at us. Orders, I've learned, are screamed, as if our ears were plugged with candle wax.

I was kept running about the ship and busy, dodging chickens with every step. Did glance at the steep reddish-yellow cliffs as we sailed through the Golden Gate and into the Pacific. Thought about Pa, his hand raised and about to hit me. Shook the thought from my head and told myself that my life back there is dead. Then it was back to work.

The only break came an hour later when we assembled at the front of the ship for a talk by Captain Blaine. The crew is a great mix — Irish, Scot, Swedish, and Dutch, along with a number of blacks, most from South America. Do not recall much of what the Captain said as I was as worn out as a kitten. We were assigned to a whaleboat and I wound up with York and Frenchie and another greenie — a tall skeleton of a fellow named Stephen who wears the most gloomy expression on his face — in the second mate's boat. There are four whaleboats on the *Florence*, which are suspended over the sides of the ship and ready to lower at all times. The second mate — Mr. Lewis — and our harpooner — Joe — were just then steering the ship, so we did not get to meet them.

Next, the common seamen were divided in half for the watches. Each watch is four hours long, with half the crew on watch and the other belowdecks. The exception is something called the dogwatch, which has all of us on deck between four and eight in the p.m.

Captain Blaine seemed distracted and jittery, his eyes blinking constantly. Reminded me of my father after a long several days of drinking. Don't waste food, Captain Blaine told us, or you'll be put on half rations. No fighting. No whistling as it might scare off whales. Obey orders and don't talk back, etc., etc. Everyone will have a trick at the wheel and I expect you to box the compass in a week's time.

I was wondering what that last part meant when the Captain suddenly came alive. "I mean to be fair," he said firmly, "but I won't let anything interfere with taking whales. Remember that while aboard my ship."

Then off he went to the aft of the ship and we were put to new tasks with Mr. Green's usual words of encouragement. The *Thomas John* was in front of us and Mr. Green was boiling angry that we were trailing in her smoke. Did not help that several men on the *Thomas John* shouted rude things in our direction, which got our harpooneer Joe screaming about modern contraptions such as steamships.

Was never so glad as when the bell rang to signal the end of our watch. Just before going belowdecks, I searched behind to see the mainland growing smaller and smaller. There is no going back now.

Later still

Our next watch will be called soon, but I want to tell about my first shipboard meal. When I ended the last entry, the door to the midships burst open and the cook made his appearance, trailed by the cabin boy who was carrying two large buckets. The ship's cat scurried in, too.

Cookie wore big black boots that weren't tied up, so he thumped whenever he took a step. "Grub's as ready as it'll ever be, ya worthless — . Eat up and no back talk ne'ther."

Most greenies were too seasick to eat. Nathaniel prayed that the world would stop spinning and Stephen amen-ed that several times in a voice that could have come from the grave. A young sailor — his name is Ethan Braddy, I think — went around with a repulsive old piece of salt pork dangling from a string saying the cure for seasickness was to swallow it and have it pulled up the throat slowly. His smile widened when any of the greenies gagged.

The lurching of the ship and the lurching of my stomach did not make me eager to eat, either. But then my day's old hunger won out. Dug out my metal bowl and spoon and joined the line to be served.

Held out my bowl and Cookie ladled in some mysterious chunks of meat from one bucket, all of it swimming in a thick, greasy gravy. The cabin boy — he's called "boy" by everybody so I don't know his name — pulled a hunk of stale bread from the other bucket and plopped it on top of the food. He scowled hard at me when I said thank you.

It was still very early in the a.m. and this was not my notion of a proper breakfast. But Cookie did not look as if he wanted to hear my opinion, so I kept my thoughts to myself. York, Frenchie, and others had plenty to say about the food — none of it good. Cookie looked offended and said, "Ya wouldn't know fine grub if ya went facedown in it!" which got a big laugh from the men.

Sniffed suspiciously at my breakfast as it had a biting burnt smell to it. Then raised my spoon to my lips. Was so awful-tasting it made me gag, but I choked it down and took another spoonful. And another. Next moment I was gulping it all down — one, two, three — then I wiped clean my bowl with the bread and devoured it, licking my fingers at the end.

That was when I looked up to find many of the men laughing at my "table manners." Cookie said it was good to see someone who appreciated his cooking besides the cat. Frenchie commented that I ate like a starving wolf cub. So now my bunkmates call me Wolf. Wonder if I will lose my memory of the past as easily as I've lost my name?

May 10

It is Sunday. No labor is done on a whaler on the Sabbath
except sailing the ship and keeping lookout for whales —
for we hunt every day. A few hours after the last entry the
clouds darkened and we entered a gale. We've been in it
ever since. Rain falls endlessly and huge waves toss the
ship around like a child's toy. By late p.m. the first day of
the storm, the *Thomas John* had disappeared, lost in the
dark, boiling gray clouds that surround us.

Frenchie said it was "nothing but a bit of weather" and
I must say the officers and able seamen act as if all is calm
and usual. But to us greenies it is as if G——d is stirring
up the ocean to make us suffer for our sins. I know I have
plenty of sins to repent.

The chickens were all chased down into the midships
of the *Florence* and put under Cookie's care. Hard to tell
who is making the bigger fuss, the chickens or Cookie.
Makeshift pens were assembled on deck and covered by
a large piece of canvas so the pigs and goats wouldn't
be washed away. No precautions are taken for the crew
when on watch, however.

Much groaning, blubbering, and loud praying by greenies and Stephen is curled up on the floor and completely
still. Not even a bucket of cold seawater could make him

stir, though Frenchie checked and said he was still alive. Ethan continues to offer his salt pork cure.

Happy to say I am not so bad off as the others. I found that as long as I eat my grub — can't quite call it food — I get around pretty well. Frenchie said it was a sign that I am a born sailor, which made me feel proud — until York snorted and said that was a lot of bunkum, though he did not use that exact word.

The storm and the bad condition of the greenies did not relieve us from our work. Nothing does, I was told, except a broken bone, split skull, or the loss of a finger, toe, or other vital body part. And death. So out we went — Stephen had to be kicked to get him up — to take in or let out sail, depending on the strength and direction of the wind.

On the second day of the storm the rain let up enough that we were set to fixing harpoons to wooden poles and sharpening the darting lances. We did this while sitting in the middle of the ship next to a brick structure called the tryworks where oil is cooked out of the whale blubber.

Frenchie said the harpoon is stuck into the side of a whale and the implement's evil-looking barb cannot be pulled out, no matter how furiously the animal shakes. The harpoon is attached to a long section of whale-line tied to our whaleboat. When the whale is exhausted, it is brought to the surface. That is when it is killed with the lance, which is an iron spear with an edge as keen as a surgeon's lancet.

Some greenies said they couldn't wait to get their first whale, but holding the harpoon made me less eager. Kept wondering what it would be like to have it jammed between my ribs and not be able to get it out.

Cannot relate more now as our next watch has been called. My new world moves along very quickly and does not allow much time to think over what has happened or what might happen. In many ways I am thankful for that.

Later

Rained heavily during our watch in the p.m. Came in soaked through and cold. My only other change of clothes is drying on a line strung across this room so I will spend the night shivering in these.

Still much groaning from other greenhorns, with Stephen the worst. He hasn't eaten in days and the skin on his face clings very tightly to the bones beneath. He looks worse than when I first saw him, if that is possible.

I haven't described the second mate, Mr. Lewis, yet. He is of average height, somewhat thick in the body, but very strong. During the worst of the storm a rope for a sail was yanked from the hands of two sailors and Mr. Lewis grabbed it up with one hand, his other being occupied with his pipe. He held on to the rope easily even with the wind tugging at the sail until the two sailors were able to retrieve it.

Mr. Lewis has not yelled or hit anyone so far this voyage. He tells us what he wants done and we do it. Even York seems uneasy around the second mate so I asked Frenchie about it. Turns out that York sailed with Mr. Lewis sometime in the past and had a run-in with him, only to learn that the quiet Mr. Lewis packs a very loud punch.

Mr. Lewis puts me in mind of Sean Michael. Not that Sean Michael is strong, because he isn't, even though he is two years older than me. In fact, Sean Michael is frail and often sick. No, it is the quiet, thoughtful part I mean, and the way both of them stay calm even when no one around them is. Sean Michael doesn't say much, either — which is smart around my father — and he was always trying to get me to do the same.

But I couldn't, of course. Keep my mouth shut.

Sometimes Pa would be fine for weeks and weeks. Going off in the a.m. to Davidson's Coffee Import Company over on Pollard Place where he kept the account books, coming home in the p.m., asking what we had done that day and such. Like any other family, I suppose.

Only we aren't like other families because our mother

is gone. She died fourteen years ago on the day I was born, so it is just Sean Michael, me, and Pa. Eventually Pa would get sad thinking about Mother and missing her and it would begin all over again. The drinking, that is.

My heart is racing from writing the above because I know where the story always goes. Those first few drinks would lead to more, and eventually Pa would come home staggering and angry. About his work and Mr. Davidson — that he isn't fair to him because he's Irish, that he isn't paid the same as others. About how I hadn't cleaned up the rooms enough. About this and that, it didn't seem to matter. I would do my best to ignore these slights. I knew that to say the house looked clean to me could earn me a good screaming at. Besides, I didn't like to see Sean Michael upset. But the criticisms would keep coming at me and I would feel my anger coiling tighter until I'd say something back.

Guess I hoped he'd see how upset I was and stop his criticizing. Only it never worked. He would always say more — as if trying to get me angry. Pa would shout — he could raise a roof for such a small man — and sometimes accent his words with a sharp smack if I wasn't quick enough.

Why couldn't I keep my mouth shut like Sean Michael? Why did I always have to cause trouble?

May 12

Weather has cleared and we've entered calmer seas with a fresh wind to blow us along. Stephen and the other greenies are a bit better — at least none ask to be thrown to the sharks that always trail us. Nathaniel said a prayer out loud to thank the Almighty for stilling the waves and no one shouted him down.

Practiced lowering and rowing our whaleboats in the a.m. First, we loaded our thirty-foot-long boat with gear — three harpoons, three lances, two tubs with 1,800 feet of whale-line in them, a keg of drinking water, a keg of biscuits. On and on the list goes.

Joe told us why he does not use a modern bomb gun to put a harpoon into a whale — a long, rambling tale about guns exploding in men's faces and so on. After a time, Mr. Lewis took his pipe from his mouth and said, "Joe is trying to say he prefers to harpoon a whale by hand. I will add that Joe is the best at his job on the seas, bar none." Joe smiled so big I could see every one of his teeth, including the broken ones way in the back.

Then the four of us, along with Joe and Mr. Lewis, boarded and the boat was lowered to the water. Hardly seemed possible that the whole affair could stay afloat, but it did.

We pushed away from the ship and began rowing. I pulled the stroke oar, which is the shortest and lightest oar on the boat, because I am the shortest and lightest. My job, I discovered quickly, was to row and not much more. Once when I looked over my shoulder to see where we were heading my oar skipped over the water instead of digging into it.

Fell back, landing in York's lap, and received a sound slap in the head from him as a reward. Mr. Lewis took his pipe out of his mouth and told me to mind my business because catching a crab — that is what I had just done — could cost the boat a whale and possibly our lives. Then he told York not to hit me again.

I set my mind to rowing after this, but still caught a crab now and again. Stephen did, too. Both of us got scolded by our rowing mates, but no one struck us.

This is how the hunt goes. We lower and row a little from the *Florence*, then set a small sail. Usually we don't have to row unless there is no wind. Mr. Lewis stands at the back of the boat and steers us on to the whale. The fifth oar is pulled by Joe, who is at the front. When we get close to a whale, Joe sets down his oar and takes up a harpoon. His job is to stick one or more of them into the whale. When the whale is exhausted, Joe and Mr. Lewis change places so Mr. Lewis can kill it with the lance.

We practiced until my hands were bloody raw and throbbing. Then we headed back to the *Florence*, a tired and quiet group. Mr. Lewis said, "I've seen worse," which seemed like high praise. He looked at York and added, "And no problems this voyage, Mr. York. Am I clear?" York nodded yes, but his face was not happy. Believe I will stay well clear of him for a while.

Later

Another hour of boat practice in the p.m. Wrapped my hands in rags this time so they did not hurt as much.

When we got back, Frenchie had me write a letter to his sister, Belle, who lives in Monterey, a tiny town south of San Francisco town. It was a very short letter, which was good because my fingers ached painfully. Seems Frenchie had left on this voyage and forgotten to give Belle the $5 he owed her. He put the money in the envelope and added another $5 as well, saying she should buy something nice for her three children. The letter will be taken by another whale ship going back to San Francisco town where it will be posted. We will do the same for others when we head home. May write Sean Michael to let him know where I am.

May 13

Boat practice in the a.m. and p.m. When not rowing, we are working on the *Florence* in one way or another — scrubbing the deck and whaleboats, untangling ropes and so forth. Also spent time in the main topgallant yard with Frenchie looking for whales. We do this while standing on a tiny platform near the top of a mast, with nothing but a thin iron hoop to hold us in place.

His only instruction was to watch for a plume of water vapor shooting to the heavens. That will be a whale blowing through its spout hole. So I watched and watched and saw nothing except blue sky and gray-green sea.

Frenchie told me that Captain Blaine has had two bad voyages in a row, and three of his last five. He took only twenty-six whales in those three. The other two made a profit for the company, but only barely. So Captain Blaine is sailing with a great weight on his shoulders. "He will either fill the ship's belly with oil," said Frenchie, "or he will be fired as Captain."

I saw nothing while aloft except a few gooneys sailing along effortlessly with their great wings outstretched. Not ten minutes after we came down, smoke was spotted on the horizon and a half hour later the ship was identified as the *Thomas John*.

Later

Calm sea tonight with a good breeze. Not much activity this watch, so the mates have let the men smoke their pipes on deck. I'm sitting in our whaleboat while writing this.

Very clear sky with thousands of stars out. Used to search the sky with Sean Michael on such nights. We would climb out the window on the third floor where we had our room and lay back against the slanted roof with our feet in the wood gutter. It was quiet there and safe and the sky spread out in every direction.

That was where Sean Michael brought me after Pa and I tangled. Look at the sky, he would say. Look at the stars and calm yourself.

It worked, too. If I was scared or angry, or if my father had just smacked me and my face stung, I would soon forget it all looking at those tiny, faraway lights.

It was from that roof that I thought to go a-whaling, too. One night, my father came up the stairs, his feet heavy and clumsy. He wasn't boiling angry when he came in and only muttered a few complaints about the food. I was able to keep my mouth shut, but I watched him closely. He looked out the window and sighed, said something about how unfair it all was, then sat quiet for the longest time.

He was thinking about our mother — the distant, sad

look on his face told me that. I thought he was lucky to have any memory of her, even though it made him sad. Neither Sean Michael nor I have any recollection of her. Wasn't even a tin image of her about. Then Pa looked at me and said, "It didn't have to happen, you know. Shouldn't have."

That was all he said, those few words. But I knew what he meant and they stung as much as any slap. She had been frail and sickly, like Sean Michael. If I hadn't come along — if I hadn't been born! — she wouldn't have died, is what he was thinking.

I was brooding on this — that it was my fault — while up on the roof that night. He didn't mean it like that, Sean Michael said. He's just sad. But Sean Michael hadn't seen his eyes the way I had. That wasn't sadness I saw. That was hate.

I looked down the hill, over the shingled rooftops, and saw the mastheads poking up above the buildings at the wharf. And here and there, hanging in some of the masts, were signal lights. Each one peaceful and still — like the stars above.

I'll never get to the stars, I reasoned, but those boats are just a walk away.

Next thing I was thinking of sailing off on one of those ships. Of being gone and not being scared anymore and not reminding Pa of what I cost him and Sean Michael.

Maybe there would be quiet in the house then. Maybe Sean Michael would have some peace.

The moment I thought that, I knew I would do it. For Sean Michael. So I settled back that night and looked at the sky for shooting stars and felt my tense muscles relax in a way they had never done before. A week after I told Sean Michael I needed to take a walk and two hours later I was aboard the *Florence*.

I am going to write a letter to Sean Michael and ask him to forgive me for leaving. He is better off now that I am gone, but I still feel bad for not saying good-bye. Then I will be out of his life forever.

May 14

Took my trick at the wheel — which is just a sailor's way of saying my turn — in the p.m., with Mr. Lewis looking on. The wind was favorable, so Mr. Lewis said to watch the compass and not let the needle drift off the point it was on. Which seemed simple enough.

Watched that needle like a hawk watches a fat mouse. Every time the needle wiggled left or right, I yanked the wheel in the opposite direction. The first few times I did this, the ship swayed and rolled as the sails lost wind.

"Easy, mister," Mr. Lewis whispered as he readjusted the wheel and the sails filled again. "Relax your hold there, son. You're not wrestling a cow, now are you?"

"No, Mr. Lewis," I answered. But I was so nervous I still jerked the wheel hard enough to get a loud rebuke from the Captain down in his cabin.

Still, Mr. Lewis let me steer the *Florence* and said I was doing as good a job as any of those below had done, and in many cases even better. He also explained the thirty-two points on the compass and said that knowing them instantly is what boxing the compass means. So another mystery of sailing was made clear to me.

By the time my trick at the wheel ended I was doing a fair job of holding the ship on course without losing wind. Noticed when I went below that my shirt was wringing wet with sweat.

May 15

Wind died away during the night and we are sitting still in the ocean bobbing like a cork. The *Thomas John* came alongside and her Captain — Captain Shubael Gardner — was rowed over with an officer to confer with Captain Blaine.

Watty Turnball wondered if they were discussing the lack of whales — have not sighted a one, which he says is unusual. Cookie said the mates chased him away from Captain Blaine's rooms, so he could not hear what was being said.

This started a great deal of talk in the forecastle — talk and complaining being the chief hobbies down here. Most feel it is a serious matter that we haven't seen any whales. Even some greenies offered up opinions. Nathaniel said that if G——d had ordained that we would take a whale, it would have happened, and that there was no use being upset. Angry mumbling greeted his remarks, but did not quiet him. Opened his Bible, he did, and read about ships going to sea to hunt the Leviathan: "'These all look to Thee, to give them their food in due season. When Thou givest to them, they gather it up.'"

That proved it, Nathaniel said — G——d gives when He decides the time is right. And clearly the time isn't right for us.

By their looks most are still not convinced, feeling that a good captain will always find whales. But no one dared challenge the words of the Bible. Then York went over to Nathaniel's bunk. Show me that saying, he demanded, and when Nathaniel pointed to the lines, York leaned over and looked at the page very carefully.

I remember the ship rolling gently back and forth several times, issuing creaks and groans as York read those lines to himself. Knew he was reading because his lips were moving. Then he grunted softly, and — faster than a blink — he ripped the page from the book and tore it into shreds.

Don't know what possessed me, but when I saw this I shouted for York to stop. Maybe it was his blaspheming the Holy Book. Maybe it was the shocked-scared look on Nathaniel's face. Like Sean Michael's when Pa explodes. Or maybe I am always bound to make trouble.

Doesn't matter why, I guess. I did it and York turned on me, his face a hard, stern vision.

Called me a "runty potato eater" and wanted to know what I'd said. His voice was so angry it seemed to shake the beams and planking. York was all coiled rage ready to strike, so I held my tongue until my brain began working. Then I said it was just that he had ripped the Bible and the Bible was blessed.

So what? York wanted to know. The forecastle was very still, with York glaring at me. After a little while, I shrugged. When he saw that I was not going to challenge him anymore, York grunted to dismiss me and turned back to Nathaniel, letting the torn pieces drop to the floor like falling snow. "No more Bible quotes," York said, "unless they bring us whales, you hear?" Yes, Nathaniel said, clutching his book to his chest.

The tension lifted and talk went back to what Captains Blaine and Gardner might do if whales stay scarce. I sat quiet — not wanting to provoke York further. At one point when York was talking to his mates, Watty leaned over to me and whispered, "Ya did good, lad. That one with the Holy Book there hasn't the sense o' a bedbug."

Later

After a long palaver the Captains emerged and orders were shouted. A rope was run from our ship to the *Thomas John* and we are now in tow. The going is slow, but we *are* going and that is the advantage of steam. We are also eating their smoke constantly and Joe cussed our having to rely on such a "squeaking, hissing, d——n contraption."

May 16

Second day in tow.

Belowdecks in the early p.m. some from midship visited the forecastle — Mr. Diggs, who makes our casks and sharpens the irons, Cookie, Joe, and another harpooneer. More complaints were aired — about the steam whaler and the lack of whales. Most blame the Captain for the latter, but I do not see how he is to blame since he can't direct whales to swim in our direction.

Also spent time writing letters for several shipmates. Jim Browning had one done to his sister in Boston, who is sixteen and — as he said to me — on the wild side. He told her about the voyage, then closed the letter with a dire warning: "Stay clear of the docks and wharves, dear Liddy, as the men there have no good in their hearts and little money besides."

It was late p.m. when a spout was seen some five miles off the starboard. Without a breeze we could do nothing but watch it swim and listen to Joe cuss and fume as the *Thomas John* untied us and steamed off after the whale. She chugged hard for an hour and lowered two boats. But then the whale went down and was not seen again.

Signal flag from the *Thomas John* recalled the boats and I must say I felt disappointed that the chase had come to nothing. Had spotting a whale signaled a change in our luck? I wondered. But what did it mean that the whale escaped?

May 17

Sunday again and still no breeze. Some stir at dusk when a lookout spotted a large, dark object floating nearby. Boats lowered — in the hope that it was a sleeping whale — but it turned out to be an immense tree, roots and all.

Mr. Green jumped onto the tree and pulled a small ax from its side. He said the ax was from islands near Japan and would bring us good luck, so we carried it back to the *Florence* and embedded it in the forward mast. Nathaniel did not say anything out loud, but his sour expression said he did not approve of such actions — especially on Sunday!

Began a letter to my father. Wasn't sure what I wanted to say, but after I told him I was on a whaleship, I found myself annoyed and tongue-tied. He probably doesn't care one bit, so why bother? Tore it up and wrote this instead.

May 18

The wind has returned and we are making fine headway. On our own! No whales in sight, but the mates and crew seem happier. Many believe it was the ax that brought the wind back and that soon it will bring us some whales. Frenchie is even having a new snake tattooed on to his arm to celebrate our changed luck. I'm not sure that the return of the wind has anything to do with finding the ax, but who am I to say?

May 21

Have to tell someone what happened, but am not sure any of the crew would understand. So I will have to write it down here and be done with it.

Between watches we were in the forecastle — where else would we be? — some yarning about other whaling voyages they'd been on, some reading or playing cards. Jim Browning was sending up a dismal wail from a wheezing concertina, but no one seemed to mind the noise. Noticed that two men had their faces pressed up against the wall that separates our space from midship and were talking away.

Another man joined them, peeked through the crack, then joined the discussion. More followed until there was quite a crowd jawing away over there. Turned out they were looking into a storage area containing casks of water, food, and other provisions. One cask was leaking, the men could see, and the liquid was collecting in the top of the cask just below. The excitement came when Watty sniffed at the crack and proclaimed the liquid to be rum.

How to get at the rum was the next topic of discussion. The entrance to this storage room is in the midship area and locked. No seaman can enter that part of the ship without permission from one of the mates, and no mate would be foolish enough to let the men at the rum. Stephen suggested removing some wall boards, but they are one-inch-thick white oak and nailed solid.

I did not care about the rum. Reminds me of Pa in a bad way and I don't need that. So I put my hands behind my head and stared up at the bunk above. Can't remember what I was thinking about — might have been remembering Sean Michael and the last time I saw him — when something scratched the back of my head.

The cushion we sleep on is called a donkey's breakfast, because it is a burlap bag stuffed with hay. Pieces of hay are always poking through the cloth and biting at our skin, but this time it set me thinking. Pulled apart a seam in the bag and took out some long, fat pieces of hay, then fitted two together.

I was about to suggest that a long straw might be fashioned to draw up the rum, when I hesitated. A sip of rum might send one or more of the men down the same path my pa always takes. Why would I send another man off on the same journey?

Put the hay back in my cushion and lay there, listening, as the men continued to argue. I could be the hero, I thought, by just telling them my idea. Maybe some would even become my friends. But I couldn't bring myself to suggest making a straw.

I was feeling very confused when Nathaniel sat down next to me. He said he could tell I was a good, G——d-fearing person at heart, not like most of the others down here who are sinners and blasphemers.

Was annoyed at Nathaniel for judging the others so harshly, so I asked in a sharp whisper why he had signed on a whaler if he did not like the life. He looked surprised and said he didn't come to hunt whales, but to "hunt souls for the L——d."

I was about to say something when York said, "Look, our little boys here are discussing Scripture passages."

Felt my face flush at this attention when Nathaniel made things worse. "Don't you have a church to go to?" he asked York. "Yes," York replied. "Once a year faithfully, I walk by one and am thankful I am not inside." The men all roared with laughter at this and my face flushed even harder, I am sure.

Told Nathaniel to get away from me and shoved him from my bunk. So there I was very puzzled. I had kept a commandment by keeping my mouth shut about the straw and had broken another by opening it in such a mean way.

May 24

Exhausted but want to get this down before the memory floats away. This p.m. we were riding a fair wind, everyone looking sharp for whales. Was late in the day and the sun was settling lower and lower, when Watty sings out, "Thar blows! Thar blows! Thar go flukes!"

Those below were on deck in a flash and searching where Watty was pointing. Even the animals seemed to stop and take notice. It did not take long before we located spouts and the *Florence* was bearing down on them.

Whales were off our lee side and not moving fast. I counted three spouts, but Frenchie said there were at least six and maybe eight in the school. When we were close — but not so close as to scare them — the Captain ordered the boats lowered, which was when Nathaniel said suddenly that it is the Sabbath, the L——d's Day, and the Captain shouted, "Sunday and the L——d be d——d when whales are near." Without another word we set off.

The wind blew strong, so we moved quickly toward the animals. A signal flag was run up to alert the *Thomas John* that we were chasing fish, and I saw that ship come about.

The boats raced through the water, moving apart to strike at different whales. The wind shifted when we were a mile from the ship, so the sail was lowered and we took up our oars. Sunk my oar in the water and pulled, telling myself to pay attention and not make a mistake.

Pull, pull, pull, we did, and the boat rushed along. Pull, pull, pull. I put my oar in the water, pulled, lifted it from the water, leaned and pushed to get that oar back and ready, and repeated the action. Again and again. My hands no longer hurt when we rowed and my arms felt stronger, too.

I didn't look around, though I was never so curious to know what was going on. Were we close to that whale — *our* whale? Had it spotted us yet? What was Mr. Lewis seeing when he whispered, "Slow, boys. Slow"?

Dipped my oar in and pulled and hardly a squeak was heard. Was so quiet I thought I would explode and the feeling was made worse by Mr. Lewis's unwavering stare. I gulped in some air and held it inside tight. "Stand by your iron, Joe," Mr. Lewis said very quiet-like, taking his pipe from his mouth and stowing it in his pocket.

At that moment I noticed in the distance that Mr. Green's boat was sitting still, with him at the rudder, their harpooneer standing with harpoon gun ready to fire, the crew motionless with oars raised. A perfect picture. Except there was no whale in sight! It had sounded and now they had to wait for it to reappear.

I was wondering if maybe our whale had gone under when Mr. Lewis screamed, "Now, Joe, now, give it to him!"

I jumped and at the same time I heard Joe grunt as he hurled his harpoon into the side of our whale. There was a great noise of water churning as the whale jerked and convulsed and thrashed about in surprised panic and Mr. Lewis yelled, "Take up oars! All abaft, by G——d!! All abaft!!!" which I did without a second thought.

As the boat pulled away, I turned my head slightly— just enough that I saw out of the corner of my eye a gigantic tail rise up and then snap down in our direction. A giant black shadow coming to crush the boat and me with a single blow. Closed my eyes, expecting the worst.

THWACK! That tail hit the water just beyond the tip of my oar and sent a wave of watery foam over us. Back we bounced on the wave as Joe's second iron missed its mark and down the whale went in a great bubbling froth of water. For a second the only sound was the singing of the rope as it flew from the tub, the whale swimming deeper and deeper and deeper.

Joe said it was the biggest whale he had ever got fast to and Mr. Lewis told Joe the iron was well placed. Everyone congratulated Joe and had a smile on their faces. Even York.

A minute went by, then two. The line still humming sharply. Then five. Mr. Lewis issued orders—"Stay clear of the line. And Stephen, close your mouth." Joe mumbled that the whale was going straight down and York said,

"Yes, straight to h——l" and still the rope went out. Ten minutes, fifteen.

The second tub of rope was tied to the first and it went out at the same speed for another five minutes. How deep can a sperm whale dive? How deep was the vast, dark emptiness below me? For some strange reason I chose that moment to wonder what Sean Michael might be doing and hope that he was thinking of me. Praying for me.

At twenty or twenty-two minutes the whirring of the rope began to slow, but did not stop. It kept playing out until there couldn't have been more than a few feet in the tub. Mr. Lewis told us to stand by to haul in the whale-line.

Frenchie had told me about this part of the hunt during one of our talks. When the line finally stopped we were to pull the whale back up to the surface, though how a few puny men and boys could haul that monster up was beyond me.

Finally, the line stopped and the order given. We all stood and grabbed a piece of the line, bracing our feet as best as we could against the ribs of our boat. Then we began pulling. Cannot say I felt a live whale on the rope. More like an immense dead weight.

Inch by inch it came up, painfully, slowly. The boat was no longer quiet — everyone was encouraging one another to pull harder. I pulled until my hands began to burn, my leg muscles began to weaken. "Haul away, now, men. Haul." Mr. Lewis was urging us on. He'd grabbed hold, too, and was straining as hard as any of us.

Then, suddenly, *snap*, the whale resumed swimming and the rope jerked again and pulled us forward, with me knocking into Stephen, who flew overboard and took Frenchie with him. They both surfaced, Stephen spitting out water and thrashing about, and Frenchie cussing the existence of all greenhorns.

I would have gone over, too, except I crashed into York, who was planted in the boat like a rock. He gave me a few "kind" words and a sharp elbow to the chest.

The line went dead a second time and Mr. Lewis ordered us to haul it in again. Only, when we pulled this time there was no weight at all on the other end. He might be swimming to the surface, Mr. Lewis said, let's get the line in before it tangles.

We brought the line up as fast as we could. Frenchie got Stephen aboard — with more cussing, of course — and then after we had gotten in all the line, we saw what had happened. The tip of the harpoon had snapped clean off the iron shaft and our whale was gone.

Joe got very angry and said he'd never seen an iron break like that. Mr. Lewis looked upset, too, and added his own choice words about the blacksmith who had done the bad forging.

It was dark by this time and no whale in sight, so our hunting for the day was over. Back we rowed to the *Florence*, being guided by lamps hung about the deck. During the trip Frenchie let Stephen have it for his clumsiness, with York saying it was me who had started it all.

Stephen did not defend himself, but he looked miserable. I said York was right — that I had knocked into Stephen, so it was my fault they went over and that the whale was gone. Mr. Lewis put a stop to it, saying the whale was lost because of a faulty harpoon only and that Frenchie needed a bath in any case.

Still I could not shake the feeling that I was somehow to blame.

We were a sober lot by the time we secured our boat and reported to Captain Blaine. The Captain took it all in, shaking his head about the harpoon and adding his own comments about the smithy. It did not help that two other boats pulled up then without whales.

You can imagine the long faces on everyone. The sea had been perfect, there were whales a-plenty, and they hadn't even seen our approach. But for one reason and then another we had taken none.

Talk was in glum whispers, as if there had been a death in the crew. Captain Blaine said every harpoon and lance, every inch of whale-line, everything in the whaleboats would be checked and checked again, and that the mates should look sharp this time. Mr. Lewis winced at the remark.

Joe repeated that our whale had been huge, sixty or more feet long and one hundred barrels of oil at least. Then he wondered why he had to pick up the bad harpoon first. No one mentioned bad luck, but I would wager that thought was in many heads just then.

Looked to be a very gloomy night when Mr. Green's voice cut through the darkness with the welcome words, "We've a whale in tow." Everyone's spirits lifted immediately.

We have been given twenty minutes' time to rest and take some coffee — which tastes like boiled boot — and the time is almost over now. More later.

Later

Another break, so I will continue about our whale.

It is a sperm whale and Mr. Lewis guessed it is forty-five feet long. "A runt," said York with a grunt, to which Cookie replied, "Bigger than the one yur boat brung in." The long, dark shape lashed to the side of the ship looked more than big to me.

We did not spend much time gawking at our prize. The goats and pigs were caged and the chickens chased belowdecks. The cat has been shut up in the Captain's room and cries constantly to be let free.

Soon enough we had the cutting stage lowered so the mates could get at the whale with their long blades. Jack Reden — Mr. Green's harpooneer — jumped upon his whale, a cutting blade in hand. Balancing unsteadily on the swaying and bobbing creature, he cut a hole into the skin near a fluke, after which he inserted the enormous blubber hook. All the while he was at this, the few men on the cutting stage jabbed with their lances at the sharks that tried to get at the side of our whale.

I was forward with Frenchie, Jim Browning, and Stephen, pumping one of the two handles that work the windlass. Four other men worked the second arm. When ordered, we pumped and a long chain attached to the blubber hook and running up to a mast and then back down to the windlass began to be hauled in. This action lifted up the whale and made the entire ship groan and tilt in the whale's direction.

We strained to our task, with Frenchie cussing the rest of us in regular fashion for slacking, so it was hard to watch all that happened. Besides, it was as dark as a cave by this time and the lanterns on deck did not cast much light.

I know the mates cut through the mouse-colored skin to either side of the blubber hook. We pumped more and the great strain from the hook made the whale roll over in the water, causing the skin and blubber to tear off in a huge, bloody strip. Like a giant, bleeding piece of bacon.

When this was fifteen feet long, another hook was inserted close to the whale's body and the strip cut free. This blanket piece — which Frenchie guessed weighed 2,000 pounds — came flying over the rail and was dumped on the deck, still oozing blood and oil. Men there set upon the piece, chopped it into smaller slabs, and dumped them between decks into the blubber room, where it was cut into even smaller pieces.

A second blanket piece was cut and went soaring over the rail. There was a screamed warning, but too late, and the ton of blubber hit Nathaniel — who was probably looking to heaven and not to his task! — and sent him sailing across the deck and into the opposite railing.

Men nearby stopped to watch Nathaniel stagger to his feet with a dazed expression on his face. He slipped in the gore that had spread across the wood planks and went down again in a sprawling heap. Everybody went back to their tasks and Nathaniel had to get to his feet on his own. When he finally did, his clothes were crimson red with blood and oil. Mr. Green shouted for him to look lively and Nathaniel moved along in time to avoid being hit by the next blanket piece.

The tryworks were alight by this time and the first cut-up pieces of blubber sizzling away in one of the two copper pots. A sharp, biting smell filled the air — the stink of burning blubber — and black smoke belched from the tryworks, coating the nearby rigging with soot. The hot oil that was cooked out was piped through leather hoses down between decks where it cooled in copper tanks and then was stored in giant wood casks.

We took in several more blanket pieces when the call came that the head was ready to be brought aboard. This was done in two stages — the first being the lower half of the forehead called the junk. Next came the case — the upper part of the head, some fifteen feet long and so heavy that as it lifted from the water the ship leaned over until the deck scuppers were level with the sea. When both pieces were secured on the deck, Mr. Lewis said Stephen and me needed a change and put us to bailing the case.

A cut had already been made in the top of the case and some oily matter scooped out. Now Stephen and I were ordered to strip and climb inside the head. Did not exactly rush to take my clothes off.

"Don't worry, it's dead," said Mr. Lewis, and when we dawdled he added, "Hop to it, men. The pot is waiting."

Got my clothes off and that was when the strangest thought came into my head — "Now, this is like stepping inside a great, huge cow." I'd hunted a whale and had it slap its tail at me — I'd seen this particular whale dead and floating alongside the ship — seen the blubber sliced and torn from its side — seen the deck strewn with oily slime, blood, and bits of skin — but not until this moment did I think of the creature as more than something to kill and cut up.

Once the idea was set in motion it was hard to shake. The day before, this mass in front of me was alive and swimming about the ocean with its family. Then along we came and stuck a harpoon in its side.

While I thought this I walked up to the case — which was taller than me — stepped onto a cask placed next to it, and tried to look inside. A lamp was hanging nearby but did not cast much light into the dark hole. Just do it, I ordered myself, and so I slithered up and into the whale. My toes sank into a soft, spongy matter, still warm to the touch, and unmistakably something once alive. It touched my legs and back and arms and made me shiver.

Do your work, I told myself. Don't think about it. People back home need the oil for their candles and to keep their machines oiled and running. And every drop of oil means more money in your pocket. A bucket was handed to me and I dug it into the side of my small space until it was filled with an oily mass. Passed this out to the waiting man, Ethan Braddy, who handed me another bucket for filling.

Stephen had joined me and together we worked, knocking into each other with greasy elbows and knees and such. Do not know what Stephen thought, but I moved as fast as I could so I would be done soon. The feel of the oil all over my body, in my hair, nostrils, and mouth, did not sit right with me.

Don't know how much time went by while we were at this task. A half hour or more without a let-up. And since Stephen is not one for talking, it was a quiet time.

Which meant I set to thinking — about the whale, and then about Sean Michael and my father. Does Sean Michael miss me? What does Pa think of my leaving? I'll bet he's happy I'm gone. At least the house is quieter now.

I was handing out a full bucket and probably thinking too much about home when my bare feet slipped and that bucket went forward and out of my grasp. The next second I heard Ethan shouting as the bucket caught him square on the top of his head. Then he was screaming at me, oil and little bits of white matter all over his face.

I think my pencil would burst into devilish flames if I wrote what Ethan called me. Let me just say it was blistering and I guess I deserved it. Still it didn't stop me from laughing, he was such a sight, which only intensified his rage.

Mr. Green came by and yelled at me, too, though not because he was taking up for my oily helper. He was angry that I had wasted a bucket of spermaceti, which fetches a higher price than regular oil. Then he was yelling at both of us for dawdling, and I was soon passing buckets to Ethan again, who grumbled with every exchange.

When we finished Mr. Lewis sent Stephen and me belowdecks to clean up. I wondered what Sean Michael would say if he'd seen me naked inside a whale shoveling out oil.

The cutting in and boiling went on throughout the night and into the dawn, with only brief spells to rest, eat, and change jobs. After bailing the case, I worked in the cutting room, then helped Cookie bring great slabs of red whale meat to the galley for our next meal. Cookie told me I would like the taste of whale steak, especially with his special rum-and-molasses mixture. Said I couldn't wait.

When all of the blubber had been removed, the intestines were searched for a substance called ambergris that's used in making perfume. Then a shout went up to haul away the chains to let the headless, peeled white body of the whale float away. The moment this was done, the sharks moved in to strike at the body from every underwater angle. Screaming birds descended and began picking with dangerous sharp beaks at the remains above water. Even an hour after, I could see a black cloud of sea vultures circling above their meal.

May 26

Finished boiling late a.m. today. Tired and sore, but we made thirty-three barrels of oil. Nathaniel's shoulder became stiff and he had to work one-armed until the first mate saw him and ordered him below.

Ethan is still angry about his oil bath. I tried to pass the accident off as nothing very important. Ethan didn't see it that way and said something back about me that I did not like and won't repeat here. The next instant we were yelling at each other and about to exchange punches, only several of the crew broke us up.

The whale steaks tasted surprisingly good, if oily. Some said it reminded them of veal, but I have never had that so I cannot say. To celebrate, Cookie also made plum duff. It contains flour, potash, drippings of hot whale oil, salt, raisins, and sugar — *but no plums!* — all boiled for several hours. A chewy sweet ball, though I much prefer crackle from the try-pots — blubber cooked in oil until it is crispy and golden brown. Now that is a real treat!

Wrote a letter to Sean Michael about our whale and such, but decided not to mention Ethan. Do not want him to think I am causing trouble here, too.

May 27

We have been kept busy cleaning and scrubbing the ship of our first whale and keeping watch for our next one. Checked all gear until the mates were happy everything was in good shape.

Spotted a sail on the horizon and we came about to speak her. It was a clipper ship, but she would not slow to exchange news or pick up mail even though we signaled her. Cookie got a telescope to make out the ship's name, but she was too far off. All Cookie could do was shake a fist at the disappearing ship and cuss it roundly for being un-neighborly.

May 28

Two days of foggy drizzle and no whales. Ran alongside the *Thomas John* and the Captains exchanged a few shouted words, then broke off. Their crew looked sullen, I think because we took the first whale. Not many days until Hawaii, we're told, where it is hoped whales will be more abundant.

Nathaniel's shoulder and side are a livid black-and-blue where the blanket piece struck him. He has trouble lifting his arm and does only light chores. The cabin boy will take his place in the first mate's boat if we raise a whale.

Nathaniel says his injury is a message from the Almighty to repent our sin of whaling on the Sabbath, etc. York said he should shut up about repenting and pay better attention when on deck.

Mr. Diggs — who is the closest thing to a doctor we have — brewed up a poultice of minced chicken intestines, vinegar, various powders of tree bark, and ashes and applied it to Nathaniel's injury. If the stink down here is any indication of this plaster's worth, Nathaniel should be cured by morning. Or dead from the smell!

Ethan still mumbles when I'm near. He believes I dropped the bucket on purpose. Watty says to ignore Ethan and he will eventually run out of steam. Sounds like good advice, but I have never been very good at ignoring insults, big or small.

May 31

Gammed with the whale ship *Mary*, just from Hawaii, with Captain Rodmann. I set to writing Sean Michael another letter, but others began clamoring for my writing services. I made my letter brief, but did ask to be remembered to Pa. Not that he will care.

Did four letters for bunkmates. Jim Browning sent one to a Miss Esther Spanner, who is a friend from his church. Nothing unusual in what he said in it until the last section where he suddenly apologized for "that most awful situation that developed between us, which was my doing and not yours. If you can forgive my weakness I can rest happy at night again." Wanted very much to know what had happened, but Jim seemed so embarrassed by this part that I just handed him his letter and watched him hurry off with it.

Ethan does not say much to me anymore. He just stares hard. Maybe Watty is right. Maybe Ethan's anger is drying up at last. Still, I find his looks annoying and wish he was on the other watch and out of my sight.

Later

Several of the *Mary*'s crew visited our ship during the gam. Exchanged newspapers and books. Our mail was rowed over in a burlap bag when some of our crew went to the *Mary*.

The *Mary* has been out nearly twenty-nine months, sailing the Hawaiian, Australian, and Japanese waters, but is returning with her hold only half filled with oil. Whales — especially sperm whales — are scarce everywhere, it seems.

Talk developed about why this is so and there were many opinions on the subject. One says they have swum off to other seas and are hiding from us. Another thinks they have taken to living underwater during the day and come to the surface only at night.

The truth is that whalemen have many ideas about whales and are happy to share and argue loudly over them. But I can't say that any of what they say sounds convincing. They know how to hunt whales and how to cut up and cook them, but on the ways of a whale, they use phrases like "I reckon" and "I think it so" too much to be believed.

Talk soon turned to sea stories and what a lively time was had. Watty told one about a swordfish that rammed the side of a whaler so hard that its long, pointy nose went right through the thick hull and stuck a sleeping sailor in the backside. The fish died when it struck the ship, and the Captain worried that to remove the nose would cause a terrible leak. So it was left in place for the remainder of the voyage. The sailor recovered, Watty explained, but he never had a peaceful night's sleep after that, not with the sword always tickling him in his aft section.

I wondered if this was a made-up yarn and asked Watty. "As true as any tale you'll hear on a whaler, lad," he said, "and maybe more so."

At dusk, the *Mary* broke off and headed for home. Many of the men sighed and wished they were aboard her. Must say the thought of home made me wish I was aboard the *Mary*, too. Strange. When I was there I wanted to be away and now it is the other way around.

June 3

We have been in tow behind the *Thomas John* for two days now. Some shouted insults from her crew with ours asking how many whales have they taken recently. Whale spotted in the a.m., but turned out to be a Sulphur-Bottom, so neither ship chased it. Too fast for even a steam whaler, Frenchie told me, and Sulphur-Bottoms sink when killed.

Captain Blaine has not been on deck in several days and an uneasy, brooding silence has taken hold in the forecastle. As if any noise would scare away whales. York wears a face that would turn milk sour. When someone asked why he is so grumpy, he snapped, "I didn't sign on for a nice sail. I signed on to take whales and make money!" Every day we see flying fish, porpoise, swordfish, great teeming schools of glittering silver fish, dolphins, and sharks — all sorts of things that swim in the sea. But no whales of the right kind!

Nathaniel's injury is a little better, but he still has trouble moving his arm. Some think he is faking to avoid heavy work, but his discolored skin — it is now a sickly yellow-green-blue — says his injury must still be painful.

I have not had much to do with Nathaniel since I pushed him from my bunk. Few talk with him anymore, even to ask how he feels, and even the pious — yes, there are a few down here — do not like his eternal preaching. He must be very lonely, I thought, especially with his arm in such bad shape.

So I went over to his bunk and asked if Mr. Diggs's poultices were helping any. Some, he said, "but prayer is the real salve." Then he asked if I wanted to join him as a soldier in the L——d's army, promising I would be rewarded in heaven if I did.

Should have prepared myself for this, but when I heard the words they still annoyed me. Said no immediately and loudly then went back to my bunk.

I felt bad immediately. Because there he sat in his bunk, looking very small with a hurt look on his face. May have even reminded me a little of Sean Michael after Pa has been on a tear. Took a deep breath and went back over for another try.

I told him right out that I did not want to join anybody's army and didn't want to talk about the Bible, either. Then — because he reads only his Bible — I gave him a newspaper I had and said he might like to read it. He took that paper warily — as if it were a sinful thing — but he did say he would look at it.

We chatted a little after this, but it was not easy. He doesn't seem interested in talking about his past or his family, and when I mentioned how warm it is now that we are nearing Hawaii he could not resist saying the forecastle is as hot as the devil's furnace. He is a strange one, Nathaniel is, but I guess no more than others down here. Including myself.

Later

I am lucky to be able to write this. I was going up the forecastle ladder when I saw a fast-moving shadow above me and pulled my head away. A bucket of sudsy water went right past me and crashed onto the ladder near my feet, sending water every which way. When I recovered enough to shout, I found Ethan on deck near the hatch, a mop in hand and a smirk on his face. "Oh," Ethan said after Mr. Green asked why I was making so much noise, "it was just an accident."

No one believed him, not even Mr. Green, who told Ethan that he will stand an additional watch. Ethan protested but Mr. Green said this would teach him to avoid such "accidents" in the future. Then Mr. Green told us to all go about our business. Only I'm not sure I can. That bucket came too close to splitting my skull open.

Later still

And if it had I would never see Sean Michael again! Or my father. That last thought has kept me awake many hours now. Why did I think of Pa, I wondered, when it was him that drove me away?

June 6

Wind returned and we have set sail again. Feels good to be free of the *Thomas John*. Many other ships in sight now. Frenchie says this means land is not far off. Nathaniel returned my paper and said he found the various stories enlightening, though he did not seem inclined to talk about them. Have a feeling he didn't approve of all he read but that he did not want to make me angry by saying so. He has resumed some of his duties now, though working in the rigging and rowing are still beyond him.

Have ignored Ethan all day, though I flinched several times when I thought he was behind me. At least Pa makes noise when he is angry!

June 8

Can hardly believe what took place even though I was not many feet away. After breakfast a lookout spotted a whale a mile or so from the *Florence*. The *Thomas John* was well ahead of us so we lowered two boats, ours and Mr. Le Page's, who is the first mate.

The wind was good so we made steady progress to the whale. The whale was slapping at the water with its tail and I'm sure the noise this caused helped us approach undetected. Seemed like we would have our second whale in the space of fifteen days!

Mr. Le Page's harpooneer attached the first harpoon. The whale thrashed its tail, swam around in a circle, and even snapped its massive jaws several times.

Mr. Le Page's boat backed away from the angry monster, while Mr. Lewis maneuvered us about so we could put in a second iron. Down under the water the whale went, then almost immediately it reappeared, wiggling and doing what it could to throw off that harpoon.

The whale dove again. Almost immediately the line

went quiet and a second later one of the men on the boat shouted a warning, pointing down. But it was too late.

The whale struck the bottom of Mr. Le Page's boat with the front of its head and the impact snapped the boat in two as its giant body flew up and out of the water. Heard the sharp report of the boat splintering into pieces, the shouts of the men, Mr. Le Page roaring an oath at the whale. Saw equipment, whale-line, casks, sail, and men all soar into the air.

The whale hit the ocean and a bubbling shower of water shot up, making it difficult to see. Then Mr. Lewis had us rowing hard toward where the shattered remains of the whaleboat floated. We had one man pulled from the water within moments. This was Josh Nichols. He'd been right under where the whale struck and the force had tossed him nearly fifty feet in our direction!

Most of the men could swim, but one named Collins had been knocked unconscious by a flying oar and was being held up by Mr. Le Page and another man, who were both clinging to a portion of the debris. As we approached we could hear Mr. Le Page calling to us, "The boy. See to the boy. He's gone under."

The boy turned out to be the cabin boy. He'd gotten snagged in the line and the last Mr. Le Page saw he was being pulled under by the fleeing whale.

Spent the rest of the a.m. and most of the p.m. searching for him. The remaining whaleboats were launched to help, and the *Florence* cruised in a circle with men in the masts watching for the boy or his body. The *Thomas John* joined in the search, too.

All day we looked for the cabin boy, hoping he'd gotten free. Called the boy's name over and over, too. He'd always been referred to as "boy" before this, but now I learned that his name was Richard Colter and that he was just twelve years old and very proud to have replaced Nathaniel at the stroke oar.

June 9

Both the *Thomas John* and the *Florence* had sea anchors out all night and resumed the search for Colter at first light. Saw nothing but the rolling sea. Gave up around noon. The *Thomas John* stood by as our crew assembled and the Captain read a prayer for Colter from the ship's dusty Bible.

After this, the *Thomas John* made steam and headed for Honolulu. Our men were allowed to stay on deck for an hour where they talked about Colter in quiet voices. Jim Browning said Colter put every effort into his rowing and Mr. Diggs said he always jumped to whatever task was given with great energy and good cheer.

Must say, I recall the cabin boy as a grumbly unpleasant sort, though I did not put voice to this thought. Others remember Colter in a different way now that he is dead and I did not think it fit to say otherwise.

Cookie brought a great pot of coffee on deck and went around pouring for the men. Cookie recollected that Colter was a good boy who had signed on so he could make money for his widowed mother and three younger brothers. "He shoulda been playin' in the street like others his age. But now . . ." Cookie shook his head.

Then Ethan added, "Wasn't even his oar to pull, ya know." No name was mentioned but most eyes swung in Nathaniel's direction.

June 11

Have made Honolulu on the island of Oahu. The harbor is very large and home just now to thirty-eight vessels, whaler and merchant alike. A few of the merchant ships are from places like Spain and France, but all of the whalers and most of the merchant ships are flying the flag of the United States.

The crew should be buzzing with talk about visiting town, but instead all are quiet remembering their missing shipmate. I feel sad, too. Colter was never very warm to me, but he never tried to hurt me, either. Still, I did glance at the land nearby and felt a twinge of excitement.

Honolulu, I can see, is of fair size, but not very big when compared to San Francisco town. A jumble of light-colored buildings with the smoke from cooking fires trailing up to an intense blue sky. It is the mountains and forest behind the town — giant shoulders of shimmering green dotted with flashes of brilliant reds and yellows — that make my head swim. If only Sean Michael could see them.

Wished I could stand there looking at the scenery, but we had work to do. A ship, Frenchie was quick to point out, is a creature in need of constant attention. So we stood our watches as usual, cleaning, painting, repairing.

The *Thomas John* is anchored nearby and Captain Blaine and Mr. Le Page have gone there. Had not set eyes on the Captain since the crew gathered to pray for Colter, and I was shocked to see his face so pinched and troubled-looking, his color pale.

I wondered if Colter's death has been particularly hard for him. Watty said maybe, but he suspects something else has added to his gloom, pointing out the whalers anchored closest to us. The Captain, explained Watty, can see that they are all riding high at anchor.

At first I did not understand why this would upset the Captain, but then it came to me. None of them are heavy with oil.

Later

I was part of a crew working in the lower hold where there is a leak in the side of the *Florence*. After we finished, I went to my bunk to change my sopping wet pants. Found a fish — very much dead and stinking — in it. I was so angry I might have rammed that fish down Ethan's throat if he were there. Thought to seek him out, but then I stopped myself. The mood on board has been very hushed since Colter's death and I didn't want to be the one to break the peace.

Tossed the fish into the slops bucket and turned my straw mattress over. Can hardly smell the fish what with all the other smells drifting around down here. Then I went to help store supplies below. Decided that ignoring the whole thing would probably annoy Ethan more than if I called him out about it.

Made my way through a section of the hold filled with casks and passed Ethan, who smiled right at me as if to dare me to say or do anything. Didn't bother with him at all — said hi to the man next to him, then saw Nathaniel by himself and went over to him. The watch had just been given a break while waiting for the next boat to arrive and Nathaniel had taken himself off to sit on a bag of flour.

Since he seemed to take no notice of me as I came over I asked him where his thoughts were. "The cabin boy's death," he whispered so the men nearby would not hear. He then explained that G——d took the firstborn of the people of Egypt as a warning to let the Israelites go free. He had taken our youngest crew member as a warning to repent our sins.

I'd prepared myself for something like this, so I didn't get angry this time. Told him he sounded as if he was looking forward to us being punished, but he shook his head and said that wasn't true. But the crew needs to put aside its sinful ways because "we can't escape for long, Wolf. Our time is at hand."

Nathaniel's whispered words must have traveled farther than expected because Ethan said Colter would have escaped if Nathaniel had been at his oar. "He'd be here with us if you wasn't shirkin' yur duties."

Nathaniel went to protest and so did I, and, of course, Ethan said more back, and things got pretty heated. Mr. Diggs appeared and told us to quiet down, then ordered Ethan to help on deck. Thought that might be the end of it, but as Ethan left he said to Nathaniel, "Don't worry. Your time is comin'."

June 15

We are in Waimea Bay on the island of Kauai. Here is
how we got here. Captain Blaine and Mr. Le Page returned
from their gam with the *Thomas John* in a great hurry the
other day and had our anchor up and sails set in a flash.
Do not have to tell you how the crew responded to this.

Turned out that while visiting the *Thomas John* another Captain came aboard and told Captains Blaine
and Gardner that smallpox was spreading through town.
The town has imposed a quarantine — the sick cannot
leave their homes and sailors on shore are not allowed to
leave Honolulu. The latter so the fever will not spread
to the ships.

The other Captain said there was also a rumor that
soon all ships would be quarantined in the harbor for
thirty days. He was leaving as soon as he got his crew
aboard and advised us to leave now before it is too late.
That is why we slunk away like criminals and are here
today.

The *Thomas John* had to stay in Honolulu to take on
coal. Used up most of its supply towing us, and we were
close enough to see they were pointing at us with very
angry faces. Joe was happy about this, saying it showed
the limitations of steam and the superiority of sail. All I
know is that we are to meet the *Thomas John* somewhere

else in a few days — if she is not quarantined, that is — but none of the mates will say where.

So we are here taking on salt pork, vegetables, blasting powder, and other necessities. The boats fly from the ship to the tiny town of Waimea, load up, and fly back to unload. Captain Blaine has gone to visit the one other whaler anchored in Waimea Bay to discuss the whereabouts of whales, but left word that he wants everyone jumping. He worries that if the authorities in Waimea learn we have been near Honolulu we will be held here a month.

June 16

Work has gone so well that we will be allowed to go ashore, two boats at a time. Mr. Le Page's and Mr. Green's went first — Mr. Le Page because he is first mate, Mr. Green because his boat took the first whale. But their leave is almost over and then it is our turn. Can tell you the spirits aboard have gone up and we work with a new determination. Oh to feel solid ground beneath my feet again!

Later

Ten or so of us were belowdecks helping stow away the supplies when a boat bumped into the side of the *Florence*, followed by a sudden commotion on deck and hastily given orders. After a few minutes, the boat left.

Those of us below thought it might have something to do with a quarantine. Pretty soon we could hear the thumping of Cookie's boots as he came along a passageway, down a ladder, and along another corridor. Then Cookie appeared and told us some men have run off, but he couldn't get close enough to the mates to hear any names. The Captain is being called back to the ship and Mr. Lewis is very serious.

Later, after dark

Those on leave were brought back — those they could find, that is — and everybody assembled on deck to count heads. Seven men are missing, but Mr. Diggs reminded the mates that two of these men always get very drunk and always turn up when sober. That means only five have deserted — Jasper Gibbon, Buck Riffs, a third man who goes only by the name Bembo, plus Ethan and Nathaniel.

I said that couldn't be so — that Nathaniel wouldn't desert, especially not with Ethan. Most agreed with me, but the fact stands that Nathaniel is not aboard. Captain Blaine told us we would search for the men in the a.m. and that all leaves are canceled. When some grumbling met this order the Captain said, "Talk to your shipmates about it when we get them back."

Men drifted down the forecastle ladder but no one went to sleep. Most thought the deserters were smart to get away while they had a chance — the ship being cursed, a man dead, and so little oil to show for our time out.

June 17, early a.m.

Mr. Green's boat went out to search for missing shipmates, with some borrowed men from Mr. Le Page's crew. Mr. Green is so angry that he can barely say a sentence without sputtering and trying to hit someone. The rest of us are bringing the remaining supplies aboard and stowing them away as quietly as possible. We had no breaks at all, except to gulp down a cup of coffee. The entire crew has been punished for the sins of a few.

It was in the early p.m. when Mr. Green's boat approached the *Florence* with an extra man aboard. When they tossed a rope up, I saw that it was Nathaniel. What a sorry figure he made as he was shoved from the boat to the rope ladder and slowly made his way up to the deck. Everyone stopped to gawk as Mr. Le Page went over to meet him and Mr. Green said, "Here's this one for you. I've already talked to him some." That was when I noticed the side of Nathaniel's face was a livid red where Mr. Green had struck him.

Captain Blaine appeared next. He did not say much. Asked Nathaniel where the others were and when Nathaniel shrugged his shoulders, the Captain suggested that Mr. Le Page and Mr. Green continue the questioning belowdecks. Then Nathaniel was shoved toward the hatch to the midsection, where he and the mates disappeared.

The rest of us were ordered to get back to work, which we did. A few minutes later Mr. Green came back up and, after speaking with the Captain a moment, got into his boat and headed to shore again. Later, Cookie came around with coffee and news. Seems Nathaniel will get three days in the lower hold in chains with half rations. He would have got more time below but he told the mates where the others are hiding without any trouble. "Told them right out, he did," Cookie said. "And they didn't even hit him once. Can you imagine that!"

This was the talk in the forecastle, of course. I said I didn't blame him for talking what with Mr. Green ready to pound the facts out of him, but I didn't find many backers. Even Frenchie said he should have held out.

There is more to this than Frenchie says — those in the forecastle work, argue and fight, complain about the food, wash clothes, write letters, and do all manner of other things together, much as a family does, so keeping a secret is expected. I never said anything to anyone about my father's drinking even though neighbors asked why my eye might be swollen or my arm bruised, so I understand this.

Thought about this some more and I guess I wouldn't talk — not if it meant getting Frenchie or Watty in trouble. But I'm not sure I would take a beating for Ethan.

Middle of the night

Mr. Green's boat returned accompanied by some loud voices. York was at the forecastle hatch and said he saw Bembo and Ethan brought aboard. Bembo was cussing and saying vile things and his hands were bound tight in front so it was hard for him to climb. York thought Bembo's face was badly bruised, so he probably put up a fight. Ethan wasn't tied up and York couldn't tell if he'd been struck. They disappeared belowdecks for questioning, which went on near an hour. No one knows what happened, but Mr. Green did not go out again. Where is Cookie when we really need him?

June 18

Got our news with breakfast. Ethan and Bembo are to stay below at half rations for seven days. Gibbon and Riffs avoided capture and fled into the forest and the Captain does not want to waste time looking for them, worried that the authorities in town might quarantine us. Would have left this a.m. except that the wind blew straight in off the ocean so we are trapped in the harbor. We're bringing aboard more fresh water, while Mr. Le Page goes ashore to find our two drunk shipmates and to sign on replacement hands for Riffs and Gibbon. There will be no replacement for Colter and this does not sit well with Cookie.

Later

The Captain let us assemble on deck to get out of the heat below. Mood is very dark among the crew and Nathaniel comes in for most criticism. Thou shalt not snitch seems to be the first commandment among the crew, while deserting is a lesser sin.

Cookie was grumping about having to take food and water down to the men in chains. I volunteered to help out so I could see Nathaniel and find out why he deserted.

Went below with a bucket of food and another of water, moving as carefully as possible through the dark passages. There are no lamps in the space occupied by Ethan and Bembo, so it is a terrible tomb to be stuck in for a week. Ethan wanted to know what I was up to when he finally realized who was serving him his meal, but I told him to be quiet and put a full ration of food onto his plate. Bembo didn't even bother to look at me as I did my work, but he did glance up when he saw I was putting a full ration on his plate, too.

Nathaniel was being kept in a tiny space at the stern and was asleep when I pushed open the door. The noise got Nathaniel stirring and when I asked why he'd run off, he really came alive.

He didn't, he insisted. He'd gone looking for a missionary's church he'd heard about and spotted Ethan and the others go wandering by. He thought something was odd when the group walked right past a grog shop without even pausing, so he trailed along, thinking he might be able to preach a little of the Bible to them when they got to wherever they were going. Which made sense coming from Nathaniel. The long and the short was that Ethan and the others went into the forest to a house with a bright blue door that was guarded by a large, hungry-looking dog. Nathaniel can deal with sinners, but not with a dog, so he went back to town, got all turned around in the streets, and missed the boat to the ship. Mr. Green wouldn't believe that he hadn't deserted. He said that to miss the boat back was to desert so shut up and he smacked poor Nathaniel to help him remember this.

I asked why he'd told Mr. Green and Mr. Le Page where the others were. Nathaniel looked at me as if I were crazy. He said that at first he wasn't going to talk because he thought the Captain a sinful man for whaling on Sunday. But once below and facing Mr. Green he decided that deserting is an even bigger sin.

I left shaking my head over Nathaniel. Watty is right — Nathaniel has no common sense. So little that now he will have to answer to all of the crew for his actions.

June 19

Did my chores for Cookie. Got the same warm greeting from Ethan, though this time he asked if I'd spit in his food and Bembo told him to shut up and not to give me any ideas. Told Nathaniel that there are hard feelings about him among the crew and that he better be prepared when he's released tomorrow. He did not seem upset, I guess because he assumes G——d will watch over him. I did not mention the discussion in the forecastle about him that ended with York saying, "Accidents happen on whalers all the time."

Some time ago Mr. Le Page returned with the new hands. One is a boy my age or a year older whose name is Monsoon, if I heard correctly. He was put in Mr. Green's boat and I certainly feel sorry for him.

The one to replace Gibbon is something altogether different. To begin, he is well over six feet six inches tall, and powerfully built besides. And black as the night. We have many colored in the forecastle with skin ranging from a deep olive to a rich, dark chocolate. But this new hand is black in the truest sense. Yet it was not his height or skin that stopped talk on deck. It was his clothes.

He wears bright yellow pants that reach only a little below his knees and tie at the waist with a white sash. His vest is blue with white stripes and open in the front revealing a broad chest. On his head he wears the most outlandish hat I've ever seen — white fur with an array of big green and blue feathers stuck in it.

As he strode across deck to the forecastle hatch he received a barrage of whistles, hoots, and insults that he did not respond to at all. As he neared the hatch, Frenchie said, "You are strutting like a peacock. Maybe that should be your name here. Peacock. How does that suit you?"

The new hand looked Frenchie square in the eyes and replied, "I am called Joe."

Frenchie acted shocked and said Joe was just not a fancy enough name for someone decked out so colorfully. But this new Joe said again, "I am Joe."

That was when our harpooneer Joe elbowed his way through the men to confront the new hand directly. I think our Joe began this conversation as a joke, hoping to add to the new hand's discomfort. There followed a remarkable exchange that went as follows:

—"No fancy-pants peacock is going to be Joe, you hear? I am the only Joe aboard the *Florence*." (After saying this, Joe looked around, smiling at the men.)

—"No, I am Joe also."

—"And I say you're not!" (Joe said this in a very firm voice.)

—"But I am. When I was baptized my mother called me Joe and when I signed papers today I signed my name Joe. So Joe I must be."

—"You don't understand. I am the real Joe around here." (Joe was growing annoyed by this time.)

—"I am Joe here and everywhere."

—"We can't have two Joes, you . . ." (and our Joe rattled off a string of impressive cusses). "It'd be too confusing, you . . ." (and he repeated his string of cusses, adding a few new ones for good measure).

—"I am called Joe. You can be Little Joe." (Which was true. Our Joe is almost two heads shorter than the new hand.)

—"Why you . . ."

But Joe — for that is what we call him now — just walked away and ignored our Joe's comments. Besides, the men on board had changed their tune, swayed by the new hand's cool composure. Now they began baiting our Joe, saying things like, "Hey, Little Joe, how's it feel to be bested in a duel of words by a man who only uses a handful of 'm?"

Our Joe grumped off, cussing. Even though some of the older men now call him Little Joe, I still call him Joe to his face. But in here, he will be Little Joe from now on. Must say it was good to have the men distracted and laughing again.

June 20

Finally set sail today in the a.m. and are making slow progress toward the Tropic of Cancer in a very light breeze. Uneasy feeling on board, but no one has mentioned Nathaniel today or unfortunate accidents that might happen.

Ethan quieter, thanks to the eternal darkness of the hold, I guess. Did mumble something unpleasant about "whispering secrets to my pal the snitch" as I left.

Later

Nathaniel released when the dogwatch was called. Cookie had me delivering coffee — made with the same coffee grounds he used yesterday and the day before! — and I noticed that the men seemed to stay clear of Nathaniel. Chatted with him when I gave him his coffee and made a point to tell him to be careful, especially when aloft. When I went to continue my deliveries, York stopped me and said, "Best be careful around that one, Wolf."

June 21

No wind and we are once again idling about in the water. A steam engine would come in handy just now.

The new Joe is in the first mate's boat and Mr. Le Page gave him some clothes from the slops chest and ordered him to change out of his colorful outfit. He and Monsoon seem to know their way around a whale ship so they are no burden to their shipmates.

Because there are no whales and the sea is so calm, there was not much for us to do while on watch. So Mr. Le Page set us to getting the ship in prime shape. Again! If ever I get back home, Pa will not be able to criticize the way the house is cleaned, that is for sure.

Was mopping the aft deck, working the mop back and forth across the — to my eye — already clean planks. Glanced up and took in the busy deck — men mopping like myself, others painting and caulking a whaleboat, Mr. Diggs sharpening cutting implements. Then I spotted Nathaniel tucked in among a small group repairing sail.

No one was talking to him — but then again, hardly anyone talked with him before. At least he hasn't said anything out loud about the Scriptures. I'm sure that would set some of the men off in a bad way. Of course, eventually a Bible quote will come out of his mouth.

This actually got me upset for getting involved with *his* problem. Why couldn't he take care of himself? Why did he always have to say and do what he thought was right and get others involved?

I plunged the mop into the bucket and sent a shower of water splashing across the wood planks. Mr. Le Page told me to be more careful, so I bent to my task and swung the mop more slowly. Of course, nothing I think about Nathaniel matters very much now. I am involved and that is that. Just like Pa is my father and there isn't much I can do about that, either.

Later

Was at the wheel in the late p.m. with Mr. Lewis. The wind was light but steady, so I could keep us on course and still look at the stars and worry over Nathaniel at the same time.

Wanted to say something to Mr. Lewis about Nathaniel, but thought that would be like snitching. On the other hand, if it is Nathaniel against York and who knows how many others, how can that be fair? It would be like my father taking after Sean Michael with me not there to defend him.

That last thought settled it. I waited until I was sure no one was near and then mentioned Nathaniel's problem to Mr. Lewis.

Mr. Lewis whispered that I didn't have to say any more, that he would take care of things, but that I should keep my ears and eyes open and report anything to him directly. He did not ask for any names, which was a relief.

Went back to steering, my mind freer for not having all that about Nathaniel bottled up in my head. Mr. Lewis wandered off to check on the forward-most whaleboat, leaving me alone for several minutes. He's left me to steer by myself more often recently and I take this as a sign that he trusts I will not do anything stupid.

Very quiet on deck — could hear the slap of water against the hull, the creak of masts, some murmuring voices. A peaceful time, like being on the roof with Sean Michael. Wonder what he is doing? And how he and Pa are getting along? If they are. Tried to picture Sean Michael in my mind, which proved to be harder than I'd thought. When I sailed, I had promised myself that I would put thoughts of home aside, but I do not want to forget my brother so completely.

When my watch ended, I sat against the tryworks, not wanting to enter the stuffy forecastle any sooner than necessary. Mr. Lewis spotted me and asked if I wasn't tired and when I told him why I delayed going below he nodded and said, "Enjoy the warm weather while you can."

When I asked what he meant he said, "Just that, Wolf. There's a cold wind in our future." The way he said it was almost like a warning.

So there I sat, looking at the stars. Had signed on so I could find that calm feeling inside, but here I am on a troubled ship, with a grumbling crew and a captain who can't find whales.

Glanced around and saw the ocean running on in all directions. A great big emptiness. Though the air was very warm and sticky, just then I felt a chill deep in my blood.

June 22

The wind is feeble, so even with all sails set we are making slow progress. Weather is clear but extremely hot and dull, which weighs heavy on the crew's mood. When I told Mr. Lewis's words to Frenchie, he grumbled, saying it is clear we will be heading to the Arctic.

Most do not look forward to the cold and want to know why we don't go down to Australia or New Zealand. A few vowed to imitate Gibbon and Riffs and run off. Grumbling about our trip to colder regions developed into a stew of the usual complaints.

The one good part was the men were distracted and did not say anything about Nathaniel. In fact, I was beginning to think it would all pass when York had to say, "Let's not forget the Bible-boy."

My visit to Ethan and Bembo was uneventful enough — a glance when I opened the door, a grunt when I said to hold out their plates, a cuss about the quality of the food. As I was closing the door, Ethan suddenly blurted out,

"Tell your pal that I'll be looking for him in a few days, hear? Tell'm that." Bembo nodded in agreement.

Said tell him yourself or something clever like that, but the hate in Ethan's voice has me worried. No telling what might happen to Nathaniel with those two after him and the rest of the crew happy to ignore it.

Later

In the early p.m. Mr. Lewis suddenly appeared in the forecastle. He said we needed to make some changes and went on about how tall Joe is and how small the bunks. Then he moved several men about so that Joe has two bunks side by side to stretch out in. Because this left us one bunk short, Nathaniel has been moved to midship. Both Joe and Nathaniel looked very happy as they bundled up their gear. Do not think it an accident that Nathaniel was the one moved.

As Nathaniel took his things toward the door to midship, one man joked by saying, "Let us know what real food tastes like." Then another less friendly voice said, "Don't think you can escape the forecastle forever." It was York who glared at Nathaniel so fiercely that I thought Nathaniel might cry.

June 24

Sighted the small island of Nihoa, which is maybe four or five miles across, and the Captain brought the ship into a tiny harbor. Sitting there waiting was the *Thomas John*. She'd gotten clear of Honolulu before any quarantine was imposed, then steamed past us during one of those windless nights while we were lolling about going nowhere.

The crew of the *Thomas John* was already at work, rowing back and forth from ship to shore, bringing aboard firewood, sweetbreads and coconuts, and fresh water.

We were set to the same tasks, which was hard work with the sun beating down on us. Several hours later the Captains met for a talk and when this ended, the *Thomas John* made steam and then chugged off. Watty noticed she was headed north.

We stayed the night and finished bringing aboard what we needed. Then Captain Blaine ordered the anchor raised and sails set. He wanted the ship to be moving under full sail as quickly as possible, adding that we have a lot of time and a lot of whaling to make up. We, too, headed north, the cold Arctic clearly in our future. Those not on watch went below murmuring softly among themselves. Myself, I went up the rigging with Watty to watch for whales.

Watty was very quiet, which was unusual. I did little real watching for whales. Mostly I thought about Nathaniel and the awful situation he is in.

If I had been able to go ashore with him back on Waimea Bay I might have stopped him from following Ethan and the others and then none of this would have happened. 'Course, that would never have happened since we're in different boats, and yet I still beat myself up over not heading this off somehow. And I could have been nicer to Nathaniel. Should have been. I should have put up with his endless Bible talk and preaching and not abandoned him to work things out himself. It is too late now. He has been branded a snitch and is trapped on board.

June 25

Cookie reported that Nathaniel is sick and has puked several times. Has a headache and a fever as well. "That's what he gets for eating your chow" was the general comment. The mood changed when Stephen — looking as ghostly as ever — wondered if it could be the smallpox.

This prompted a lot of worried discussion and speculation — the latter mainly about being stuck at sea with an infected man. Mr. Diggs tried to reassure the crew, saying that it couldn't be the smallpox because no one went ashore at Honolulu. But the crew was not much relieved.

Later

Ethan and Bembo released. Came up during the dog-watch and were greeted warmly by the crew. Ethan — who may be more foolish than Nathaniel — demanded to know where Nathaniel was and said he was going to teach Nathaniel a lesson with his fists, etc. Mr. Green was there in a second and told Ethan to shut up or he'd be in chains again. Ethan started to talk back, but Bembo grabbed him and pulled him away. Thought I heard Bembo mutter, "Don't worry yourself. He can't hide for long."

June 26

Nathaniel continues ill and the crew continues to be restless about it. Ethan suggested that Nathaniel be put off the ship, land or no land, and no one argued very much with him.

June 28

Two days rainy weather and strong winds. Jim Browning lost his grip and fell from the rigging in the early a.m., but was fortunate to get caught in a sail — which slowed his fall — then land in a whaleboat on top of the sail.

He is mighty banged up with many cuts and bruises and a very sore head. Nothing is broken that we can tell. Mr. Diggs is brewing up another of his foul-smelling poultices so we have spent as much time on deck as possible, rain or no.

In the late p.m. Nathaniel came up on deck to take some fresh air. It was dark but still I could see he was sickly. Did not see any pox marks on his face or arms. Asked him how he felt and he said his head still hurt and he needed to get back to his bunk. As he went toward the hatch, Ethan said, "Scurries like a rat."

Nathaniel stopped and turned just as Ethan took a step toward him. When I saw the scared look in Nathaniel's eyes, I stepped between him and Ethan and told Ethan to leave him be, that he was sick. More words followed, of course — most of which I cannot write down here — but I was happy to see that Nathaniel slipped down to his bunk in midship.

Mr. Lewis has begun teaching me how to navigate and take readings. This requires a great deal of adding and subtracting, which makes my head swim. When I complained, Mr. Lewis told me I will need to know how to do this if I intend to be a mate. He was not joking with me, either.

June 29

Nathaniel stayed below today, sick as a dog. Those midship are now worried — this according to Cookie.

June 30

Cookie announced that Mr. Diggs consulted *Dr. Pierce's Medical Advisor* about Nathaniel. Mr. Diggs went down the list of symptoms and asked Nathaniel if he had this one or that one, etc. and put a check next to those he said yes to. Only two checks out of eleven symptoms, so Mr. Diggs still does not think Nathaniel has the smallpox. Even so, he decided not to take a chance of infecting the crew and had Nathaniel moved to a storage area in a lower hold.

July 1

Nathaniel forgotten for a while when we took a large sperm whale late yesterday and commenced cooking. Likely to make ninety barrels or more if Frenchie's guess is right.

Mr. Green's boat made fast but the frightened whale swam along giving Mr. Green and his men a real Nantucket sleigh ride. And oh did Mr. Green cuss that creature as he went flying past us. Mr. Lewis steered to head it off and a half hour later Little Joe pitched two harpoons into its side. This took all the fight out of the creature and Mr. Green had him spouting a shower of blood in no time.

Had a strange feeling as our men attached a line to the whale and its blood spread over the water until we were completely surrounded by it. Do not have proper words for it. I remembered being inside the case of our first whale and picturing it alive, and I noticed that as this one swam past us I thought its eyes looked scared. Like Sean Michael's when Pa gets loud. But it's silly to compare him to this animal.

Delivered food to Nathaniel while the cutting in and boiling went on. It is sweltering hot where he is and heavy with the smell of overripe fruit. But he seemed calm and said he uses his time alone to think about his mission, which is to save sinners. I advised him that first he has to save himself from the likes of Ethan and Bembo and this actually produced a smile.

When I went on deck to help with the cooking of the whale Ethan shouted out, "Have you been sharing secrets with your pal below?" The men all stopped their work to stare at us a moment, I think because they expected a fight.

Before I could say anything to Ethan he was ordered forward and the men went back to their tasks. I was left alone with an awful feeling — anger, sadness, confusion, embarrassment, and more, all leaving a bitter taste in my mouth. How to be rid of it?

July 2

Nathaniel is reported feeling much better, but he will stay in the storage area another day. So there is no small-pox. The mood aboard brightened after this news, but then sank again when Jim Browning had to be carried to his bunk in the p.m. He has tried to work a little these past few days, saying that anything is better than endur-ing Mr. Diggs's poultices. But today he had a great pain in his belly and suddenly his legs would not move.

Mr. Diggs thought it might be something Jim ate — maybe the salt pork we had yesterday — but Cookie insisted that he always cuts off the really bad parts of the food before cooking it. The men seem happy to blame Cookie as it makes for a good show when he huffs and puffs and carries on. Even Jim managed to smile through his pain and say a few unkind words about the grub.

I'd caught the spirit of the exchange, too — until I saw Ethan staring at me. Made myself angry when I turned my head away quickly, as if I was embarrassed. But what do I have to be embarrassed about? I will not turn away the next time!

Leak in lower hold has returned, but is not worrisome. Pump it out every a.m. before breakfast.

July 7

Took a sickly sperm whale in the p.m. It hardly moved as the first mate's boat approached and only shuddered when the harpoons and then the lance were heaved into its side. Seemed unfair — like shooting a neighbor's cow. Nathaniel took his place in the boat, but his face was all pale and sickly. Made Stephen look healthy!

Frenchie thinks we might cook twenty or twenty-five barrels from it. And so to work.

Later

We were cutting up our whale in the blubber room when mention of the Arctic started much talk. The men are uneasy because Captain Blaine has no experience in the cold region or in navigating through the ice. Watty reminded the group that it has been just three years since a fleet of whale ships — thirty-two in number — were lost to the ice. And these were all captains who'd been there before. "Some of the men tried ta walk ta safety," Watty told us, "but they froze solid after a few steps and are still standing there waiting ta be rescued." I suspect that Watty was just yarning us, but it still gave me the shivers.

July 8

Were finishing up our whale late yesterday when a cry went up and then Joe — who was standing on the stripped carcass — held something up. It was a mass of ambergris, which he had just found while searching the whale's guts.

There were many happy faces among the crew and mates. Even Captain Blaine looked pleased. Ambergris sometimes fetches more than two hundred dollars a pound and this piece was guessed to weigh about ten pounds! A number of men reached to pat the ugly lump as it was passed aboard and brought below to be stored. Looked like a slimy, foul thing, but I guess its great value makes it less so to some.

We have taken three whales now for 148 barrels of oil. Plus ambergris. Could our luck be changing? Asked Frenchie if the Captain might turn the ship around now that we have found some whales. He just laughed and said it was too late. Not with the *Thomas John* running days ahead of us.

Later

Just realized that today is Sean Michael's birthday. Set me to remembering his last one in San Francisco town. A cold day, if I recollect correctly, with heavy, dark clouds, thunder and rain.

Sean Michael loved — *loves* to read and I had found him a real storybook with a stiff cover called *With Washington in the West*. It was missing pages in the front, but started with the first page of Chapter 1 so it was almost like a new book.

I knew Sean Michael would like the story because it was about the wilderness and had some daring adventures in it by the looks of the pictures. Pa came home with a bag of candy for Sean Michael, which he shared with us after dinner.

Pa was in a peaceable mood that night and even read the first two chapters from the book out loud, stopping every now and then to say it was a cracking good tale. Sean Michael agreed and thanked me over and over again. I remember looking out the window at the rain coming down and the curtains fluttering a little and thinking it was the most peaceful day ever.

Tried to recall other good times the three of us had, but it wasn't easy. I guess because those bad times with Pa had blotted them out. But I'm sure I could bring some of them back if I really tried.

Shook the thought from my head, not sure what good it did me to think of such a long ago and faraway scene. Which was when Ethan said, "Wolf looks mighty guilty of something, doesn't he? Maybe he and the other rat have been talking too much to the mates. . . ."

He would have said more, but I was out of my bunk and on him in a flash, my fists pounding away at his face. Not sure how many swings I took or how many landed. Wasn't thinking clearly. "Say another word," I screamed, "one more and I'll . . ."

The next second Frenchie grabbed the back of my shirt and hauled me off Ethan, who had collapsed back into his bunk with his hands up to block the blows. Then Frenchie wrapped his huge arms around me and pulled me across the forecastle toward my bunk, while Watty stepped between me and Ethan. I sputtered some words I can't remember and tried to break free of Frenchie's grasp, but it was no use. So I started yelling over Watty's shoulder, "Go ahead, say it, say it, you liar! You know I didn't tell Mr. Lewis anything! You know it!"

Some others stopped Ethan as he came out of his bunk at me, so Ethan shouted, "He hit me for no reason. I didn't accuse him. . . ." Then York gave Ethan a mighty shove that landed him and Nichols back in Ethan's bunk with a thud. "Shut your mouth, you, before the mates hear. . . ."

"But he —"

"Shut it, boy!!" And in case I planned to say anything — not that I did, mind you — York spun around and said the same to me. Relaxed my fists then and tried to control my breathing, which was hard to do because of Frenchie's iron hold. By this time, Joe was standing next to Ethan's bunk, his left arm stretched out in front of it like a gate across a toll road. He didn't say anything, but he fixed York with a hard stare. Like a huge guardian angel.

It was so quiet in the next seconds that I could hear Cookie's boots thumping along until the door creaked open and he peered in cautiously. Then he asked if we needed the mates as he glanced from face to face.

Ethan leaned out of his bunk, pointed at me, and said, "He —"

"No," York said firmly. "No trouble in here."

"Need Mr. Diggs for that?" Cookie asked, pointing to Ethan. Which was the first I noticed the splatter of blood under Ethan's nose.

"No," York answered for him. Cookie left then, slamming the door closed, muttering to hold the noise down.

There was a general rush of gabble after this — one saying it was a mighty good show, another saying fights always made him hungry, a third offering suggestions on how to stop Ethan's nose from bleeding. Frenchie released his hold on me — and a great gasp escaped my lungs — then told me to sit on my bunk. Watty said I'd handled myself well. Then out of all this I heard Ethan's voice: "I tell you, I think him and that other one . . ."

"Enough!" bellowed York in Ethan's face. Which quieted the room a second time. "You got what you deserved," York added, "and if you open your mouth, you'll get more. From me. Do you hear?"

Ethan didn't respond, so York repeated his question with a clear threat in his voice and Ethan nodded. Then York looked up at Joe and asked, "Do you want something?" Joe didn't answer him. Instead, he gave York a piercing look, then returned to his bunks.

I sat on the side of my bunk flanked by Watty and

Frenchie. York came over, too, and the three stood talking about other forecastle fights they'd seen or been in.

Glanced at Ethan and saw him dabbing the blood on his face with his shirt. No one was talking with him. Not even Bembo. He sat there without a trace of his old anger or sly meanness. Just embarrassed defeat. Knew from the look of him that he wouldn't be bothering me again soon.

Felt a rush of pride, I am sorry to admit. At having grown strong with all of the climbing, lifting, and pulling we do on board. At having handled an annoying problem so easily. And at having York take my side.

Then another thought pushed its way in. I'd handled my problem just the way Mr. Green and York do. Just the way my father does.

Looked at my hands and saw them cut and covered with blood, my own and Ethan's. Cannot say I felt so full of myself then.

July 9

Some talk about my fight this a.m. while we worked the pumps, with York — my new friend?!? — saying I packed a real punch. Ethan steers clear of me and won't even meet my eyes. He still wears his bloody shirt and I feel guilty every time I see the dark brown splotches. I was happy when our watch was called and I could escape to hauling on ropes.

Jim Browning still in his bunk, his belly sore. He has tried to get up several times, but doesn't have much strength in his legs. Mr. Diggs had the Captain look at Jim and then Mr. Diggs and the Captain went through *Dr. Pierce's Medical Advisor* to see what it suggested. Jim now gets mild tea and broth with some chicken in it.

It is funny. Nathaniel got very little attention when he was clearly injured and then sick, I guess because he was always waving his Bible in everyone's face. Jim gets many visitors and kindness. Wonder who will be there if Sean Michael gets sick.

July 11

Jim Browning is dead. He was a little better in the early p.m., but worsened as night came on. He tried to rest but was fitful all through the early a.m. Then suddenly he said his belly felt on fire and he rolled into a ball to relieve the pain. Sent for Mr. Diggs and the Captain, but before they arrived Jim's body stiffened and he cried out once — a kind of strangled gasp — then he went all still. It was a little past 5 a.m. when the Captain said he was dead.

Jim's body was brought up on deck and put in a canvas

sack with some ballast stones at his feet. Mr. Diggs sewed the sack tight and then the body was placed on a long plank, which was carried to the edge of the ship. One of those helping was Stephen and when I saw his thin arms and sunken cheeks I thought he looked worse alive than Jim did dead. Strange who is chosen to move on and who is allowed to stay.

As the crew assembled around the body, York muttered, "The second to die. Who's to be the next?"

Captain Blaine appeared, looking even more nervous than usual. Am fairly certain I smelled whiskey when he went past me. He spoke a few words about Jim — saying he was an honest, G——d-fearing man and a hardworking sailor. He finished by reading a short passage from the ship's Bible: "The L——d bless thee, and keep thee; the L——d make His face shine upon thee, and be gracious unto thee; the L——d lift up His countenance upon thee, and give thee peace."

At that four men hefted the plank with Jim's body on it and placed half of it over the deck rail. The Captain nodded and mumbled, "Let him go," and added, "and may G——d forgive his sins and speed his passage to the next world." "Amen," Nathaniel said very loudly. One end of the plank was lifted and Jim's body slid over the side of the ship, plunged into the black water, and sank out of sight in a horrible instant.

It was all so quick — Jim's fall, his painful belly, death, and burial. All in a blink, really. He was joking as well as he could with others in the forecastle just yesterday, talking with the Captain and Mr. Diggs, sipping his tea. Now his body is floating down to the bottom of a cold, dark sea. Not even a stone slab with his name on it to mark the spot.

July 13

Have not felt much like writing these past days. Too many thoughts of poor Jim Browning. Too many thoughts of Nathaniel and Ethan. And Sean Michael, too. But I will try to write it down now. If something happens to me, this journal would be all of me to survive.

All was peaceful in the forecastle after the burial. We did our work, ate our meals, passed the off hours quietly. Even Mr. Green lowered his voice. Gradually, things got back to normal and some crude jokes were traded between the men, orders were shouted about and such. Then during the dogwatch when all of us were on deck, I heard Ethan say, "Nathaniel, there's an empty bunk waiting for you below."

Nathaniel looked upset and searched about for help. Then Ethan added, "It's a dead man's bunk." I was glad when Joe slid around a knot of men and stood some feet from Nathaniel, close enough to come to his aid if necessary. I wasn't certain I wanted to rush to Nathaniel's defense just then.

Mr. Le Page appeared and told the men to go about their business. Ethan tried to act innocent, saying he was just being friendly, but Mr. Le Page ordered him to stow his chatter and go below until his next watch was called.

After this, the mates made certain that Nathaniel was watched at all times, so his duties were always in the aft of the ship where the mates tend to congregate. He didn't have to climb the riggings, either, where anything might happen. Instead, he will be Cookie's helper, which does not sit well with Cookie.

I've taken to wearing two of everything because of the cold, and I can see my breath when on deck. The forecastle is downright cozy these days, even when filled with smoke.

July 21

Steady winds and calm seas these last days. Picked up a strong northerly current yesterday and the *Florence* is sending up a spray of water as she plows ahead.

Not much else happening. Ethan joins Bembo and some other men when free of work. They mutter about going north and, of course, about Nathaniel. They don't say anything about me, I think because York has included me in his group. He calls me "Wolf" instead of just saying "hey, you" or "boy."

Stephen has taken to playing Jim Browning's concertina a lot and Watty grumbles that he should have brought his bagpipes so he could show what a proper noise is. Mr. Lewis showed me charts of the Arctic and told me what we might expect there. The ship leaks and we pump. And so we sail along.

August 2

A fierce gale came on us a day ago with winds strong enough to blow the hair off a dog. The seas are big and rolling. But since the wind blows north the Captain has had some sails up and we are riding along hard and fast.

Mr. Lewis says it is dangerous work to have canvas on during a gale. A sudden gust of wind can pull a sail free or even snap a mast. But the Captain wants to make a fast passage north, and so we will chance disaster.

The mates have more men on deck than usual. Two men on the wheel to hold it steady, four men on lookout for big waves, land, or icebergs — *yes, it is that cold now!* Men down below are always dressed and ready to come up and assist in case of an emergency. Pumping goes on constantly, as the rough water has increased the leak.

Cookie has just arrived saying the Captain has broken open a cask filled with clothes purchased from the prison in Waimea. We are to put another change of clothes over the ones we already have on, with socks on our hands. Cookie explained that we will get proper winter clothes at our next stop, but he does not know when that will be.

Later

Was at the wheel with another man and struggling to hold on when Nathaniel came aft with coffee. Cookie has Nathaniel doing a lot of hard cleaning and carrying, much more than he asked me to do. I think this is his way of punishing Nathaniel.

Noticed a bruise under Nathaniel's left eye and asked what happened. He said it was a "little accident" and that I shouldn't concern myself. Would have asked more, but the wheel was tugging at my fingers and eager to spin free. I suspect more went on than Nathaniel said.

August 15

Two days out of Pribilof Islands in the Bering Sea and heading north. It is summer and *freezing cold*! No whales, but what else is new?

August 19

This a.m. a giant wave struck us in the side and put the ship on its beam ends. The wave was so powerful that Stephen was tossed from his bunk and landed on the floor with a hard knock to his head, crushing the hapless concertina besides. While some went up to take sail off before a mast splintered, I went below with others to re-arrange casks that had shifted.

Took about an hour to set the ship right and then the day went on — listening to Watty's tales, studying charts and navigating with Mr. Lewis, chatting with York and Frenchie. Went out of my way to talk with Nathaniel, not that he is seen often on deck anymore. The mates keep careful watch over him so he doesn't have any more "accidents."

Later

We began bumping into pieces of thin ice in the p.m. When the first bump sounded against the hull next to me, I nearly jumped from my bunk thinking we might be stoved and sink.

The Captain still keeps as much sail on as possible despite our near disaster. He is that eager to get to the Arctic before the hard winter sets in.

August 21

We stopped at Unalaska yesterday to take on provisions and cold weather clothes. Ships usually take on dogs and sleds as well, but we did not. Word is that they were too expensive and that we'll get them when we reach Point Barrow. Did not see much of the place, but what I saw was gray and brown with snow in places. A far cry from the warm, green islands to the south.

Our new leather and fur getups are stiff and bulky, but they're warm and nobody is complaining. Except Joe, who is so long in all directions that he was up late last night sewing on extra leather to cover his wrists and ankles.

August 22

Not much of note since leaving Unalaska. There is the ice, of course. Thousands of floating cakes in all directions, big and small, white and blinding. Fortunately, it is not very heavy. We are in company with a steam cargo vessel, the *General Grant*, under Captain William Bonam, as well as the *Thomas John*, which we met again in Unalaska.

Captain Bonam said the ice is unusually thin this season, maybe because of a series of recent southern storms. He said, too, that not many whales have been taken in recent months.

So the *General Grant* breaks a path through the ice, followed by the *Thomas John* and then us, steering a course around the bigger chunks. The *General Grant* will leave us at St. Lawrence Island and the *Thomas John* and the *Florence* will go on alone. The days seem longer now that we've entered the cold, but at least I can look back through my journal and recall warmer times.

August 24

Made St. Lawrence Island on the 22nd and took on more supplies. Have had no contact with Nathaniel these past few days. I see him moving about doing his chores so I know he's okay.

Ethan stays clear, but he and his mates whisper together more than I like. Said something about this to Watty and he told me to stop worrying. According to Watty, the mind has only so much space, like the hold of a ship, and to fill it up with worry is to not have room for good things. Wondered if I'd done this with Pa — filled up my head with the bad so I can't even remember the good? Of course, those bruises I had were real and I have to remember that, too.

August 27

We have entered the Bering Strait — where the Alaskan and Siberian coasts are closest together. The ice now is bigger — some cakes as big as a farmer's field! — and thicker. To move north, we sail around these cakes. When a channel opens up we can sail through easily. Most times, we zigzag here and there, following the cracks and openings as best as possible.

This is much easier for the *Thomas John* because of her steam engine. We have to haul in sail, let it out, and back again over and over to make all these maneuvers, so by the end of my watch I could see why steamers are fast re-placing sailing ships!

In the early p.m., the ice suddenly began moving south. When it does this it often catches on something — an island, rock, or sandbar, for instance. Then it piles up with cakes hitting others and jamming up the water in a solid pack of ice.

The *Thomas John* tried to ram its way through, but the ice is too thick here. This ice is not flat, as I had first ex-pected. It is an endless series of hills and sharp angles, some higher than the ship's deck. We are in calm water a mile from land, which is Cape Prince of Wales according to the map Mr. Lewis showed me.

Mr. Diggs reported that the natives on the cape — called the Esquimaux — are hostile to the white man, es-pecially whalers. According to Watty this is because twenty-five years ago a band of whalemen killed sixteen natives and stole their food. Wondered if Ethan has such a long memory.

So here we sit, a wall of ice blocking our way and ice cakes everywhere else, waiting for the wind or tide or *whatever* to move it out of our way. Could be an hour or a day, says Watty. Or a month.

Later

Ice in front is groaning and grumbling and cracking fiercely. Sounds like guns firing. It is moving, or getting ready to, but no one knows which way.

August 28

Ice moved off slightly during the night and opened a narrow channel. Because there was no wind today we had to be towed by the *Thomas John*. Mr. Green and Little Joe were furious about this!

Late in the p.m. the ice closed in again. From the lookout we can see that only two hundred yards separate us from open water. Crews are now setting dynamite charges to blast open a channel.

Nathaniel was moving about the deck while this was happening, bringing coffee and biscuits to those on watch. He looked melancholy, so I asked if something was troubling him. Shook his head no and looked down as he went off. Frenchie watched all this and said, "He is a strange one, Wolf. And bound for some terrible fate." Think Frenchie was warning me to steer clear of Nathaniel, but his words have made me think more

about him instead, just as being so far from home has set
me to thinking more about Sean Michael.

August 29

What a grand time we had yesterday. From 2 to 4 p.m.
we set off eight dynamite charges — great, thunder-
ing booms followed by clouds of white smoke and flying ice. Better than any 4th of July back in the United
States!

Men cheered every explosion. Captain Blaine stood on
the ship's deck frowning, probably because we only managed to blast out fifty feet of ice and there is still more
than five hundred feet to go before open water. Frenchie
said the Captain has the look of a man trapped. Which of
course he is.

August 30

Sat in ice yesterday. Set off six charges and gained only
thirty feet of new channel. Late in the day the pack started
pushing in on us, which made working on the shifting
ice dangerous. Men less enthusiastic about fireworks,

possibly because Jack Reden was struck by flying ice and may lose sight in his left eye.

Mr. Lewis said we should be able to sail straight up to Point Barrow without too much trouble at this time of the year. Frenchie heard this and grumbled that "this is a voyage of should-haves — should have taken more whales, should have stayed in the south."

Later

Wind shifted several hours ago and the channel is opening! Happened as fast as that. The *Thomas John* has steam up and is nudging the ice aside. Slow going, but we are going. Mr. Lewis thinks if the wind holds we will make open water before dark. It feels as if heavy chains have been taken off and we are free again.

September 2

We are in the Chukchi Sea some sixty miles off Point Hope, this according to Mr. Lewis's reckoning. Not far to the north is the Arctic Sea and most of it is marked "the unexplored region" on the charts. Asked if we would be going there and Mr. Lewis said he hoped to G——d not.

Then I went into the masthead on lookout with Stephen. The *Thomas John* had chugged ahead and I was scanning the sea to the west when I saw movement on the water two miles off. A second later came the spout. Only I didn't cry out. Thought about the way that whale looked as it swam past trying to shake off Mr. Green's boat. Remembered floating in its blood.

Was in the middle of these thoughts when Stephen suddenly screamed in my ear, "Thar blows! Thar blows!" and set the ship alive.

It was a bowhead whale — called that because of the curious bow shape at the top of its head. Mr. Le Page and Mr. Green went after it and put irons in it an hour later. Hardly any fight to it, either. Some swimming and thrashing, but it was all over very quickly.

The whale is fifty feet long and terribly heavy with fat. The windlass groans and strains under the blubber slabs, some of them more than two feet thick! Not the best sort of oil, so says Cookie, but there will be plenty of it. Warmer today, so we can work without being bundled up in furs.

The most curious part of this whale is the bone, the long, flexible baleen in the whale's mouth that the creature uses to catch food. There are hundreds of pieces of baleen on each side of the mouth, the longest more than ten feet in length. Frenchie said the bone is sometimes worth more than the oil and that most whalers in the north cut off the head and let the rest of the body sink to the bottom. We are taking on both oil and bone because we have so little to show for our months of work and Captain Blaine wants to fill the ship in any way possible.

Spent my time cleaning bone with a knife and bundling it up. It will eventually be made into buggy whips and corset stays. Do you think, Watty asked, that the fancy ladies who wear corsets in San Francisco town know where parts of them come from? A lively discussion followed.

Later

Had a chance to talk with Nathaniel while cutting up the blubber belowdecks. He seems resigned to his position on board. Says it lets him think about G——d and his mission on earth.

September 3

Still boiling. The *Thomas John* has steamed off north to hunt and we are to meet her in the Arctic in ten days. Nathaniel was on deck, though we did not exchange many words. I'm worried I will say something that will hurt his feelings, so I say nothing instead.

September 4

Finished up boiling and have commenced cleaning the ship. Captain Blaine broke out some rum and we all had a tin. Thought to give mine away, but the damp chill got to me so I drank it down in one throat-burning swallow. A shiver ran up and down my spine and made me blink several times. Which set Frenchie and Watty roaring with laughter. My head feels very thick and slow now. Is this what Pa feels, too? No wonder he is always in a foul mood.

Later

Fog has rolled in. We are dragging a sea anchor so we do not bump into anything, but the current is moving us along anyway. Watch is alert for ice and other ships and we are constantly checking the depth of the water.

September 6

Still in a foggy soup. Nervous Captain — nervous mates — nervous crew. The mates are for having two whaleboats tow the ship to the east so we do not drift too far north;

Captain Blaine worries this will take us too close to the shore and that if the wind comes on suddenly it will put us on the rocks. So we will do nothing for now but drift along lazily.

Later

Whales are near the ship, but the fog is too thick to see them. Mr. Lewis wanted to lower boats, but the Captain said no because he did not want to lose a boat in the fog. Could tell this did not sit well with Mr. Lewis or any of the crew on deck. The water is calm and the whales are swimming close by — so the risk is not so much greater than usual, really. York said, "The Captain's afraid. Lost without Captain Gardner at his side."

September 7

Last night a cooler breeze came on us and the fog began to lift. Still very much a ghost ship — the white mist covering the ship's deck and the men faint shadows. Noticed that when the Captain came up, Mr. Lewis moved away without saying a word. He is still thinking about the whales we could have taken.

Later

Thick, soft, crushed ice has begun pushing against the *Florence*. Some larger chunks mixed in with this, but nothing to do damage. So quiet that it is scary. I was peering over the railing when a voice cried out, followed by shouting. Nathaniel had come on deck with coffee and had slopped some on the wrist of John Kenealy — a friend of Ethan's — and Kenealy tossed the coffee in Nathaniel's face. Nathaniel said he was sorry, but Kenealy just yelled at him and carried on and shoved him back several times, until Mr. Lewis told him to stop.

Nathaniel was not much hurt — burned a little by the hot liquid, but there are no blisters. I told Nathaniel to be very careful and especially to make sure he is in view of a mate at all times. He said he would try, but that it is not always so easy.

September 8

Ice is pushing in on us. Captain had us sail east toward the mainland, then south, but ice had already formed there and halted our retreat. We are six miles from land, which is a distant smudge among the ridges of ice. Mr. Lewis was studying the expanse of ice to the northwest that is pushing in on us. "Pray for a change in the wind," he said. Ice is all around us now, groaning, cracking, and grumbling as it squeezes in closer and closer.

Later

Charges set off to keep ice from the hull. Wind has increased blowing from the west, so the blasting will accomplish nothing — this said by Watty, Frenchie, and several others.

After spending two hours chopping at ice near the hull, I was given some free time. Went for a walk on the ice to stretch my legs. This was no Sunday stroll, since the ice was tossed up here and there, some of the ridges more than ten feet tall. Even the flat sections were angled and slippery. Climbing over these ice hummocks and sliding down the other side reminded me of the times Sean Michael and I played on the big hills near our home, not that we ever saw much snow.

Went about a mile. The ship was still in sight, but was very small. Once when I went around a chunk of ice the size of a barn, I stopped and realized I was all alone. Just me, the ice, and the wind. Felt scary at first, but then I closed my eyes and thought about being on the roof with Sean Michael and looking at the stars and wide heavens.

Was heading back to the *Florence* when I spotted Nathaniel carrying a bucket of slops. And not far behind him came Ethan and Bembo, following him on the sly.

It did not take much thought to see that those two were up to no good and that Nathaniel had no idea he was being followed. Had no choice but to call out to Nathaniel and go over to him.

He seemed happy to see me, but before much could be said, Ethan and Bembo suddenly came over a jagged hill of ice one hundred yards away. Nathaniel saw them then and was instantly scared. I went up a slant of ice, telling Nathaniel to follow me.

He hurried along, slipping and sliding. Ethan was angry that I had spoiled their fun and shouted some unkind things, but I didn't stop to respond. Wanted to get myself and Nathaniel clear of them.

Ethan and Bembo hurried to catch up with us, but there was lots of ice between us and they weren't skilled at picking the best route. Still, they were gaining on Nathaniel, who was still lugging his full bucket. Get rid of it, I told him, but he did not want to lose the bucket and have to face Cookie. Instead he emptied its contents down a long chunk of ice that Ethan and Bembo were just starting to climb. Ethan and his pal cussed when those slops came dribbling down on them.

By this time, I'd reached higher ice and could see the ship. Thought to dance and sing out to get someone's attention, but stowed that idea. But I did call out to Mr. Lewis.

Said hi and waved, and even told Nathaniel to come and say hello to him. He was startled to reach me and discover the ice empty, but I just grabbed his arm and steered him toward my imaginary "Mr. Lewis." Our two pursuers stopped where they were, which was between two ridges of ice. They had no idea if Mr. Lewis was there or not, but they played it safe and headed in the opposite direction anyway.

Nathaniel said it was a miracle we escaped. I said it was a miracle he still had his head on his shoulders.

September 10

I woke to a startling sensation. A storm had developed, with sleet and heavy winds, and the ice pushed in and began to crush the *Florence* in its iron grip. The ship's bow lifted some eight feet up under the ice's pressure, and is stuck fast in that position. Since then the beams groan and moan under the ice's crushing force. Crew very anxious.

Leak has returned and pumping goes on continually. Watty said it is only a matter of a day or two before the ship is crushed completely. York is like a caged animal — pacing the forecastle and wanting to do something. But what? All we can do is sit and hope the ice backs off. And pump.

Later

Attempts to chop and cut the ice have been abandoned. It is too thick and the storm too severe. No more blasting, either, as it will cause the leak to increase. We keep lookout in the masts in hopes that — what?

Later still

Forecastle was quiet and tense when suddenly there was a sharp crack from midship as loud as artillery fire and the *Florence* shuddered like an animal dying. York was up in a flash and pounding on the door to midship to know what had happened. Eventually the bolt slid aside and Cookie opened the door. Seems a piece of one-inch-thick floor planking splintered under the pressure of the ice, but — thank the L——d! — no damage was done to the hull or cross beams. Mr. Diggs is inspecting some other beams and does not look very happy.

September 11

I was on deck in the a.m. trying to keep dry when I heard a mighty uproar of voices arguing from the Captain's quarters. Nathaniel came on deck with coffee and told me the mates petitioned Captain Blaine to abandon the *Florence*, but the Captain stubbornly refuses. Much back and forth, but in the end the mates were sent away and told there would be no change for now. The pumping goes on — the *Florence* screams horribly under the crushing ice — the storm continues.

York is for leaving the ship and most in the forecastle agree. When another plank snapped, York decided to speak to the mates on behalf of the forecastle. Several accompanied York, including Frenchie and Watty. Mr. Le Page sent them back, saying decisions about the ship are up to the Captain, and that we must follow his orders, etc., etc. They are afraid for their positions, York suggested later, when they should be afraid for their lives. And ours.

Later

Storm is lessening — winds have died down and the sky is clearing.

Later still

On watch late in the p.m. when Mr. Lewis joined me. He scanned the horizon to the east with the telescope, then conferred with Mr. Green, who was on deck also. Mr. Lewis pointed heavenward and toward the coastline. Mr. Green took the glass next, looked through it a minute, then cussed.

It seems the ship is moving northwest. We are still stuck in the ice, so the fact is that the ice is moving and we are being taken with it. Mr. Lewis does not think we are moving very fast, but he worries that the wind will increase and we might end up in the uncharted part of the Arctic Ocean. It has happened to many ships in the past.

Watty was nearby and when Mr. Lewis went off, he told me about a ship — the *Boston* — that was carried into the Arctic at forty miles a day and was never heard from again. Probably crushed out there, he said, and the men frozen on the ice.

September 12

Land is no longer in sight. Captain Blaine thinks we have drifted five miles during the night and are some ten or twelve miles off Icy Cape. He does not think this is very far, but it seems like a mighty distance to me.

More discussion between the mates and Captain Blaine about abandoning the ship. Cookie said Captain Blaine does not want to give up the oil and bone we have below. Mr. Lewis came away looking very grim indeed. So on we creep north with the ice — like a fly stuck on a giant piece of flypaper.

Mr. Lewis had us remove our boat from the cranes and we set to adding four inches of hardwood to its keel. We might soon be dragging the boat over the ice and the ice will chew up the wood like a hungry beaver, he told us. He did not smile when he said this.

Later

Wind has picked up and we are drifting faster. We are now fourteen miles off Icy Cape.

Captain Blaine came on deck toward evening. He walked back and forth without saying a word to anybody, would stop now and again and study the sky, etc. Very thoughtful. Then he said something to Mr. Le Page and went below again. We are staying put, Mr. Le Page informed us. He does not seem very happy, either, but orders are orders.

Belowdecks, a new reason for not abandoning the ship was offered up. Captain Blaine, it is said, owns a share of the ship and he does not want to see his money float away on the ice.

I will try to sleep, but my head is filled with nervous thoughts. Wish I could be with Sean Michael on our roof — in the warm night air!

September 13

Woke to word that we are leaving the ship. More later.

Later

Am beneath our overturned whaleboat with the rest of our boat crew, a canvas tarp stretched over the top and held down with chunks of ice. A cold wind is pushing under the canvas and biting at my face. Mr. Lewis said the temperature is probably near zero.

Lamp will be put out soon, so I have to be quick with

this. Had our boat off the ship and ready an hour after the order to abandon the *Florence* was given. Took a good deal of equipment and two weeks' supply of food and water. Every boat has a rifle as well. The oil and bone are being abandoned, but the ambergris has been stowed in Mr. Le Page's boat.

Boats set off in an orderly line, with ours in the lead since we were ready first. Captain Blaine went from boat to boat, worrying over this detail and that and asking repeatedly if the wind might come about and make it unnecessary to leave the ship.

The way we traveled went like this. Three men pulled the boat with a harness attached to the front, while three pushed. Frenchie is in the front with me and Stephen; Mr. Lewis, York, and Little Joe in the back. Much slipping and sliding accompanied the travel, with the boat keel scraping along and making a horrible, grinding sound. I turned back many times to see the *Florence* — my home for these last months — getting smaller and smaller until its masts finally disappeared in the early p.m.

Nathaniel is helping move the spare boat and several men went out of their way to shun him. Mr. Diggs is with that boat, too, and I think he will watch that nothing really bad happens to Nathaniel. The cat has also joined them.

The ice is piled up with no order whatever so there are

many twists and turns, hills and valleys. Sometimes we travel one hundred yards only to find our way blocked by a giant hummock, so we have to go back and find another route. There were also pools of water. None were deep enough to allow us to row across, so we had to circle them.

All of this was made more difficult by the Captain, who was constantly stopping the parade to talk to the mates about the best route to take, etc. During the fourth or fifth stop, York began grumbling in a loud voice about "all these d——d tea parties to chat." Frenchie says his feet are icy cold and paces constantly to keep them warm.

Covered about five miles when the Captain called a halt for the day. Mr. Lewis was for traveling through the night, but the Captain thinks this is too dangerous. At the rate we are going, it will be four or five days to the coast. And once we strike land no one is sure where the nearest town will be.

September 14

Stopped after going only three miles. Mr. Green's boat was being hauled over a ten-foot-high pressure ridge when a man slipped and the boat went crashing down the other side and was stove on one side. Repairs are being made now by Mr. Diggs and will take a while, so Cookie is making up a pot of coffee or something much like it on a portable stove.

The other mates are for going forward because a storm is coming on. The Captain says no, we must all stick together.

Mr. Lewis is not happy to be sitting here with bad weather brewing. Besides, the ice is beginning to grind again, the result of the storm kicking up distant waves. At one point, York was near Mr. Lewis and suggested in a surprisingly respectful voice that "maybe we might want to consider going on ourselves, sir. If it comes to that. The boys would follow you." Thought Mr. Lewis might put him in his place with a sharp rebuke, but instead he looked off and said, "It is an option, Mr. York."

Later

Made three miles when the storm came on. Strong winds and an icy rain in our faces but we kept going.

Our boat was still in the lead with the others strung out behind us for a great distance. Wondered how Nathaniel was doing — he has not done much heavy work since hurting his shoulder, plus he does not have any friends with him. The Captain sent word ahead ordering us to wait for the others to catch up. We did, but not without Mr. Lewis cussing this newest delay. York suggested we make believe we never got the message, but Mr. Lewis said we would obey. For now.

All of the boats arrived and we made camp for the night. While we were eating, Nathaniel joined us under our boat, though York and Frenchie gave him withering looks. Later as I clutched my hot coffee cup for the warmth I heard Nathaniel mumbling.

I was about to ask him what he was saying, but Stephen beat me to it. Turned out to be a quote from the Bible — what else? He whispered it to Stephen, but I could still hear it. "Then they cried to the L——d in their trouble, and He delivered them from their distress; He brought them out of darkness and gloom, and broke their bonds asunder."

Thought Stephen might say something rude to Nathaniel, but he didn't. Instead, Stephen nodded solemnly and said, "We could use having our bonds broken now, couldn't we?"

September 15

Sometime in the middle of the night the wind began to roar and lightning flashed. Suddenly there was a terrible

125

crash as the wind got under Mr. Le Page's boat and flung it over and over. It came crashing down on another boat, the men underneath yelling as the canvas sheets flew off and casks went rolling about.

A scramble followed to stop the boats from being tossed about more and to see to the injured men. Several crushed fingers for a Nantucket man named Carey, a mashed-up knee for Monsoon. One boat damaged. The biggest concern wasn't for the injured men. That was saved for the ambergris, which took several minutes to locate.

Storm quieted by morning and the Captain and mates talked over the situation. The Captain does not want anyone to get too far ahead today. Monsoon will ride in Mr. Green's boat and the Captain thinks his crew might need help getting him over the bigger hummocks. Carey will walk along, but won't be able to help move his boat.

While the meeting dragged on, York stalked back and forth impatiently and Little Joe complained about the poor quality of modern captains. Frenchie seems unusually quiet this a.m. because his feet are wet and cold. He wrapped canvas around his boots and this seemed to help a little, though Frenchie says several of his toes are numb.

Later

Have stopped to rest after making two very hard miles. Men exhausted from the struggle, but at least the storm has passed. The keel to Mr. Le Page's boat was ripped to shreds and the bottom badly damaged during this rough passage. Mr. Green's and the spare are in bad shape also. They did not put extra hardwood on their keels.

Mr. Diggs does not think Mr. Le Page's boat can be repaired, so it is going to be abandoned. Mr. Le Page will get the spare boat for his crew and the ambergris. Some men will be reassigned to other boats. No decision yet on where the cat will go.

We'll get two additional hands — Ethan and Watty. Ethan was not happy about the arrangement and hung back with his pals. So Nathaniel joined us — and York was not happy about this arrangement and told him to stay clear of him. I tried to tell York that Nathaniel was better than Ethan, but he just grunted at me.

Later still

We've begun to find areas of deep water where the ice has parted. Ice is softer here and is moving about, which makes for slow progress.

While going around a ridge, "One-eyed" Jack Reden slipped and fell into the water. He is a sorry sight now, standing and shivering and asking over and over again if anyone has dry clothes to lend him. Many of us have wet feet as well and Frenchie is limping a great deal. The ship suddenly seems like a very snug place even if it is drifting off the charts! I'd even prefer an angry night with my father over this.

Near midnight

Spent the afternoon moving across tall ice ridges. Took one hour to cover less than a mile and when the ice leveled out — that is, the ridges were only five feet tall! — the Captain called for a rest stop.

This time the mates argued loudly with the Captain to keep moving. But Captain Blaine said the men are played out and need rest and food, etc. Frenchie thinks it is the Captain who is played out and I have to say he does look very pale and his eyes seem heavy and tired. "Not tired," said Frenchie, "it's the drink. He's got a bottle stashed away in the spare boat." Watty added, "Aye, thar's spirits near. Can smell'm a mile off."

We went on eventually, but did not get far before fog rolled in and the Captain called another halt. We were well ahead of the others and Mr. Lewis cussed roundly when he heard the order. Told us to stand by ready to proceed, because he had no intention of stopping and was going to tell the Captain so. Off he huffed and then we saw through the mist a general gathering of men and heard a lot of shouting.

Our crew wanted to join Mr. Lewis, but Little Joe — who is second in command — said we should stay as ordered. So we waited, straining to hear the argument. The word *mutiny* floated our way at one point and then Mr. Lewis came marching back to us accompanied by Mr. Le Page.

The Captain has decided to return to the ship, Mr. Le Page announced, but Mr. Lewis insists on continuing. The news that everyone else was going back struck me cold in the belly. Felt myself drawn to the crowd — to the protection it might give. But then I thought that Mr. Lewis is no fool and that I am not so sure about the Captain.

According to Mr. Le Page the soft ice and fog has convinced the Captain that the ice is breaking up and that the *Florence* will be free in a few days. The Captain will not force Mr. Lewis or any man to stay with the ship. He did want to be sure none of us are being forced to leave. "We're for going," York said instantly and the rest of us nodded in agreement.

Mr. Le Page then said the Captain intends to file charges against Mr. Lewis for going against his orders and he might do the same against us. In addition, disobeying orders meant we wouldn't share in any of the money the voyage might fetch. A thick layer of fog rolled over the ice just then and Mr. Le Page nearly disappeared from sight. Know I wanted to be safe and warm in the forecastle at that moment — a feeling that passed when I thought the *Florence* might already be stoved and at the bottom.

No one said they wanted to leave our boat, so Mr. Le Page wished Mr. Lewis good luck, then he marched off through the fog to rejoin the rest of the men.

Mr. Lewis took out his compass and indicated the direction to the coast, then we started moving again. Have we made the right decision? Will we ever see the others again? Will we make it to shore? Such thoughts accompanied my every slippery step when suddenly someone called from the fog behind us. We halted, turning to see a figure coming our way. A very tall figure.

It was Joe, who looked like a terrible giant in his bulky furs. The second York saw Joe he growled, "What do you want?" Joe did not respond to York, of course. He turned to Mr. Lewis and said he wanted to join us if there was room. Before Mr. Lewis could answer, York said, "We've not enough food for you."

"There's enough food for all if we're careful," said Mr. Lewis then.

York scowled mightily and made it clear he didn't like sharing out his food with an uninvited guest. Frenchie, Stephen, and Watty muttered in agreement and I thought our little boat might have its own mutiny.

Mr. Lewis took out his pouch of tobacco, put some in his pipe, lit it, and took a long, calming puff. Finally Mr. Lewis said that he knew perfectly well we are in a hard situation, but that the only way to reach land is by sticking together and that the more hands we have the easier the hauling would be. Which made sense to me. He finished by saying that if anyone was scared about the food situation they could always go back to the ship with Captain Blaine.

He knew the last would get them. No one wanted to admit he was scared. So the men swallowed their gripes and off we went again and continued with only two brief stops to rest and eat.

Lamp is being extinguished. Mr. Lewis thinks we covered four miles since leaving the other men. The bottom of my boots are worn thin and damp. Won't last another day so I will cover them with canvas like Frenchie did.

September 16

Woke with the fog still with us. After an hour's journey the ice became very slushy and dangerous. Stephen slipped and went in up to his waist, but he insisted that we go on. My boots got wet, too, and are now heavy with ice.

Traveled until we came to deeper water where we stopped to dry off. Used our cooking pot to hold the fire, so as the ice melted the pot sank lower into it. We are going to put the boat in the water after this and Mr. Lewis added that this might be the last time to dry off until we reach land.

Later

Nine in this boat is a tight fit. Had to leave most of the supplies behind — including the firewood — but even then the water almost came to the top when we climbed in.

No wind to speak of, so we have been rowing. Fog has lifted in places, which takes some of the gloom away.

Began by following a channel of open water that went east, but this soon ended. Since then we have been going up one channel and then another until each ends. Whenever this happens there is a hearty round of cussing, while Mr. Lewis checks the compass and decides on which channel to try next. Right now we are heading north-west — away from land!

Stephen has not complained at all, but he shivers constantly. Frenchie says he cannot feel his left foot to wiggle his toes and Mr. Lewis thinks it might be frostbitten. Must quit as it is my turn to row.

Later

Light is fading — only a few minutes left to write. Still on boat, though oars have been put in the boat and we are floating lazily in a narrow channel while Mr. Lewis searches for a solid piece of ice to land on. Said he does not want to be on the boat if the ice starts moving during the night. Not sure being on moving ice sounds any better.

September 17

Woke in patchy fog with bits of light struggling through. I was up a while when the sun grew bright as the fog finally thinned. A cheer went up, but then a few minutes later another bank of fog closed in. Everybody was quiet a second. I know I was wondering if I would ever see the sun again. That was when the tall Joe pointed east and said, "Land." Which had us all up and searching, but we couldn't see very much beyond our noses.

York lit into Joe about raising false hopes, etc. Watty wondered if he might be seeing a mirage caused by the ice and Little Joe grumbled about people from warm climates going crazy in the north. Joe just said, "It is there. You will see."

Mr. Lewis couldn't see it, either, but did ask Joe how far he guessed land to be. Maybe seven or eight miles, was his answer. Which, of course, set York off again like a stick of dynamite.

Checked Frenchie's foot before leaving. Toes were completely numb, but Mr. Lewis judged it a good sign. If he had frostbite bad, his toes would be turning dark as gangrene spread through the dead tissues. Stephen has begun coughing and looks more tired than usual.

Rowing assignments made — York, Stephen, Little Joe, and myself for the a.m. — with Mr. Lewis steering. The rest — Watty, Frenchie, Joe, and Nathaniel — are tucked in among the gear as best as possible. Pushed off and began rowing at a leisurely pace.

Almost immediately, York started in on Joe, but this was cut short when Watty asked Mr. Lewis if he thought the Captain would really press charges against him. "He might," Mr. Lewis said. "He's a poor sailor and he'll want to blame what happened on anyone but himself."

I was amazed that he was talking about the Captain in this way. When we were on the *Florence* he never said anything bad about Captain Blaine. Never even hinted at it. I guess that not being part of the *Florence* anymore has freed him up to talk.

We are about to stop to stretch our legs and have something to eat. Must say that I actually miss Cookie's grub. No matter what it tasted like, it was usually warm.

Later

About our afternoon journey. After eating, we set off with Watty, Nathaniel, and Joe taking up oars, and Little Joe steering. Thought Mr. Lewis might choose Joe or York to steer, them being so tall and better able to see over the ice ridges, but I guess he decided Little Joe was next in rank and deserved to be at the rudder.

Traveled an hour and made little progress toward the land. So we got out and began hauling the boat toward the east. York and Joe supported Frenchie between them because he had trouble walking on his own. And did Frenchie ever cuss Captain Blaine for taking us into the cold north. Stephen continues to cough.

Whenever we came to a channel of water, we would pile into the boat and row a while. If we went away from land for too many minutes, Mr. Lewis had us out and hauling again.

During all this time, we could still not see land because of the fog and even Joe admitted that it was no longer in sight. York ripped into him then, insisting that Joe should admit that he'd made up the sighting. Joe said nothing.

Sometime in the late p.m. we came on a channel of water that took us northeast and parallel to land. Mr. Lewis thought we all needed a rest from hauling the boat and said we would float along a while. I felt all done in and made myself snug in the front of the boat. Made me wish for my little bunk in the forecastle.

Next thing I knew I was waking from a deep sleep to the sound of laughter. Watty was telling a story about a leave he had once in Australia and the men nearby were enjoying every minute of it. But my brain didn't listen to this right off. Instead, I heard Nathaniel and Stephen whispering.

Felt a little jealous, I admit, that they were so chummy. It was then I realized Nathaniel was saying a bit of Scripture between strokes of the oar and Stephen was repeating it back, as if trying to memorize it. The piece went: "The L——d is my strength and my song, and He has become my salvation; this is my G——d, and I will praise Him, my father's G——d, and I will exalt Him."

So he has found a fellow soldier at last. That actually made me happy. It means that Nathaniel has someone to talk to. And it also means I am not responsible for him. Or at least not the only one who will watch out for him.

We landed a few more times after this and I rowed for the last water part of the journey for the day. Clouds have rolled in and Watty predicts wet weather is on the way. Wonder what Sean Michael and Pa are doing tonight? My thoughts have turned often to them these past days, especially concerning Pa and his drinking. Has he stopped or not? And if not, have I saddled Sean Michael with a bigger problem than if I were there? Did not think about this before I ran off, but now it is on my mind.

September 18

A heavy, wet snow woke us before dawn. After we chewed on our ration of dry beef, Mr. Lewis had us load the boat for the day's journey. To make fun of him, York asked Joe if he could see land through the murky clouds. No, said Joe, but it is only "three and a half, maybe four miles away now." That got York awake and fast.

Got the boat in and we were rowing, but York kept at Joe, demanding how he could possibly know this, etc. Despite his foot, Frenchie also questioned the number, as did Watty, Little Joe, and — between hacking coughs — Stephen. I was at the stroke oar in the stern and Joe was right behind me, so when I turned around none of the men could see Joe's face, except me and Mr. Lewis who was at the rudder. Joe looked right at me and winked.

I laughed out loud, which had York wanting to know what I thought was so funny. His face was so angry that I could barely stop myself from laughing more and had to turn back toward Mr. Lewis. Mr. Lewis was smiling, too.

Eventually, York quieted down and commenced rowing again. We knew we were heading somewhat toward the land, so we rowed for a half hour before the channel ended and we had to take the boat out. And, oh, were we a wet and miserable lot by that time.

Much grumbling and cussing — what else is new? — as we hauled out the boat. This time Frenchie sat in it while we traveled. When we checked his toes this a.m., we discovered that two had begun to darken. The first signs of gangrene.

Frenchie did not want to ride. Said it was not fitting for him to be ferried along like an old man, but eventually Mr. Lewis convinced him it was for the best.

Before we left, Mr. Lewis asked Joe how far away we were from land. Thought York would explode he looked so angry. Joe sniffed the air several times very thoughtfully and proclaimed the distance to be just three miles.

York was sputtering when he said, "Now you want us to believe you can smell land, you —"

Mr. Lewis got York pushing and I must say York was so angry he put his shoulder to the boat as if he could move it by himself. Wondered if Mr. Lewis asked the question to get York pushing with the strength of two men. Even Frenchie laughed at the way York carried on.

Stopped early in the p.m. when the wind picked up and the snow stung our faces. It is nice being under the boat and out of the wet, but could use a warm fire. Feel damp all over and am amazed these pages are still dry enough to write on.

Nathaniel and Stephen talk in low voices, and I did hear Stephen say "Amen" at least once between bouts of coughing. Mr. Lewis is trying to brew tea for Stephen by holding a tin cup of water over the lamp's little flame. When mention of the land was made, Joe said, "It is not very far away." York must be very tired because he only said, "Oh, shut up," and did not even tack on a cuss.

September 19

Did not want to wake up this a.m. I was wet and cold and all I wanted to do was stay under the boat. But eventually

Watty got up and went outside — and a few seconds later he was hollering like a crazy man.

We all scrambled out, everybody asking what the problem was. I expected something terrible and so did Mr. Lewis, who grabbed the rifle in case we were being visited by a polar bear. No bear in sight — only Watty looking off and pointing.

We all turned to look. The snow had stopped, but the air was still heavy with mist. Still when we looked we could see a huge, dark shape not far away. Land, Watty said, and Mr. Lewis agreed. We'd stopped for the night only one hundred yards from our goal!

There was some celebrating then, though the cold and our exhaustion held it down. Then Joe said, "See, I told you it was near." York had recovered enough strength to cuss him a little, but I thought it a halfhearted effort.

Took the rest of the a.m. and part of the p.m. to reach and climb the cliffs — which were more than one hundred feet high — and haul up the boat and supplies, too.

Next, we gathered driftwood for a fire. Took a while to get it lit, the wood being wet, but it is burning now, sputtering and hissing and crackling loudly. Frenchie and Stephen — whose coughing now makes it hard for him to talk — get to stay huddled over the fire, while the rest of us squeeze in as best we can.

Frenchie's toes are worse. Darker in color, plus the

gangrene is spreading toward the foot. Mr. Lewis said we would wait until tomorrow to decide what to do. Meanwhile we have made the overturned boat and canvas cover as wind-tight as possible, though the smoke hole makes this a difficult task.

Nathaniel continues to whisper to Stephen when possible. Stephen looks ghastly. Watty slipped on the icy cliff rocks and banged up his knee, but is fine otherwise, as are Joe, Little Joe, York, and Mr. Lewis.

Mr. Lewis has just passed out our dinner — three hard crackers and two square inches of dried pork. Chew slowly, he advised, and enjoy every bit of it. To help me ignore my growling stomach, I am going to think about my last meal at home. It was a chicken stew Sean Michael had made, with potatoes and carrots and onions in it. Pa even said it was a tasty treat. Now to my Arctic feast.

September 20

About to set off, but will try to get down what happened this a.m.

Frenchie's toes were no better and Mr. Lewis said the worst looking ones had to come off or Frenchie might lose his whole foot. Mr. Lewis sharpened his knife on a rock, then heated it over our fire.

Mr. Lewis apologized to Frenchie for not being able to give him rum to kill the pain, then we all grabbed Frenchie to hold him still and Mr. Lewis went at it. I closed my eyes to the operation, but I could still hear Frenchie gasp as the knife cut into his flesh and then began sawing through bone. And did he ever thrash about as well, trying to break free of our hold — like a whale on the end of a harpoon! — and cussing us all loudly, but especially Nathaniel who had begun saying a prayer out loud.

It seemed to take forever to me, but really Mr. Lewis had that big toe and its two neighbors off in a flash. Then he reheated the knife and pressed the flat part of the blade against the stumps to stop the bleeding. The smell of burning flesh almost made me puke, but I managed to fight off that feeling and hang on to Frenchie, who had really jumped at the touch of the burning heat. Finally, a bandage made from one of Mr. Lewis's shirts was wrapped around the foot and we all let go of Frenchie.

I found myself in a fine sweat and everyone else, Mr. Lewis included, looked done in completely. Frenchie had stopped cussing and was gasping for breath, exhausted from his ordeal, but alert enough to say, "Wouldn't a pint of Jamaican rum be a wonderful thing right about now?" Everyone agreed it would.

As soon as the operation was over, Mr. Lewis had us jumping to new tasks. Setting the camp in order and rounding up wood for the fire. Of course this is a strange land of mostly rocks, rough, short grass, and a few — very few — stunted trees and bushes. And snow. Snow is everywhere the eyes travel and even with the sky clouded over I find myself blinking from the unusual light.

Gathering up an armful of wood took a surprisingly long time. When I finally got back to camp I learned that a plan had been worked out. Two parties will set out to find help, one heading up the coast, the other down.

Neither Frenchie nor Stephen can travel, so they will stay here. Stephen looks especially pale and sickly. Watty, Little Joe, and Nathaniel will also stay to take care of the sick and to keep the fire going, etc. The rifle will be left here, too, because Watty is a crack shot — or is this just another yarn? — and might be able to hunt up some fresh game.

Mr. Lewis and Joe will head north up the coast in the general direction of Point Barrow. York and I will go south. We might find Cape Lisburne in a day or two. Most of the food stays with the five here, but we are getting four days' rations — sixteen crackers, one pound of dried meat, and a gallon each of water. We have little other equipment — our knives, fifty feet of line, and a few matches is all we'll bring along.

When York learned I would be with him, he looked at me and said, "Don't go falling down and hurting yourself on the rocks, Wolf, 'cause I'm not going to carry you. I aim to be there and back before anybody misses us."

Must go.

Later

York said we would stop for a few moments, "so don't go writing your whole d——d life history there."

Left the boat a few minutes after my last entry, with Nathaniel promising to pray for our "safe passage and our souls." Hope he meant safe passage in this world and not *into* the next! Traveled for an hour before coming to a fast-moving river, then headed inland to find a place to cross — which took three hours! York marches forward as if hunting a stubborn whale and hardly says a word.

Made our crossing at a spot where the river narrowed and was filled with boulders and collected trees from upriver. This wasn't particularly difficult for York, who bounded across the wet, icy limbs as if working the riggings. But I slipped and nearly fell in and eventually York had to toss the line to haul me over.

York has picked up his gear and is heading off. Think I will follow him.

Still later

Fingers are warm enough to hold this pencil so I will tell what happened after crossing the river. Went back toward the shore — over very rough land filled with icy rocks and crevices and such. Sun was out by this time, which was a blessing, but it melted the snow enough that my feet were wet through after a mile and starting to numb up. Still I didn't stop or complain. Don't think York would have cared anyway.

Another mile and I found walking hard and began worrying that frostbite had my toes, too. Could almost feel Mr. Lewis's knife biting into my flesh! Said something about it to York, but he just grumbled that it wasn't time to stop, so on we went.

As we neared the coast, the land became even more irregular and it was here that I realized York's feet were giving him trouble, too. Knew this because he began cussing every time he had to climb over a big rock. Finally, I said loudly that our feet will freeze up solid if we don't dry them off near a fire.

York grumbled and cussed about my weakness and went on about my holding him up and that he'd rather have that meddling Joe than me, etc. But I noticed something else — York had stopped moving. So I suggested we round up wood and get a fire going, and York — with his usual cheerful manner — actually did.

Found a little wood nearby and York set about lighting it. While he was at this, I went off looking for larger pieces. Not much wood in sight among the rocks and what there was was wet from the snow and rain. Went about a quarter of a mile when I came to the top of a big hill. It was then I saw the most amazing group of constructions two hundred yards off. Four poles each six feet tall with what looked like a ship's bunk at the top with bundles in them. Twenty or twenty-five of them in all.

Blinked and tried to comprehend what I was staring at. Then it came to me. The bundles on the top of each was a body. A dead body. I'd found an Esquimaux burial ground.

Shouted for York. Screamed, really. I didn't think I was scared, but maybe I was a little. York came hobbling along and was just as surprised as I'd been. He thought there might be something we could use from the graves — blankets or boots or maybe some very dry wood to burn. That was when I realized that if there were so many graves right here there was probably a village nearby for the dead people to come from.

Could not see any structures for the living straight off, but then I couldn't see this burial ground until I'd traveled a little. Besides, if I was picking a place to bury dead folk, I wouldn't put it in my backyard. Said all this to York who stopped and said, "You know, Wolf, that is one smart notion you have there."

The ground sloped off heading south, and since the way east was a torture of rocks and boulders, we took the easiest route. And don't you know that after going up and down a series of hills, we finally went over one and found five stick-and-fur longhouses in the hollow below.

York hushed me immediately — not that I was talking — and pulled me back out of sight of any down below. Must confess that since setting out to find this village I'd been thinking about the bad blood between whalers and the Esquimaux at Cape Prince of Wales and wondering what sort of reception we'd get if we came across any. I was not all that eager to find out, either.

York wanted to find something — a rock or a long, pointy stick — so he would have a weapon, but I didn't want to wait. So we approached the little village cautiously, with York saying several times, "Keep those eyes of yours sharp, Wolf." I did.

The houses looked crudely constructed — poles jammed in the ground and bent until they met at the center of the roof, which was made of sticks with furs draped over and held in place with more sticks. I noticed that some of the furs were old and frayed, which was when I realized something else. There was no smoke coming from the longhouses.

We searched each structure and found them dark and cold and without anyone to greet us, warmly or otherwise. But it is clear that people have used them fairly recently — maybe within the past two months or so. I thought this because we found a small knife with an iron blade and there was no rust on it.

We decided to stay the night in the coziest house and were lucky to discover a good supply of dry wood here, too. The fire was smoky but warm. Pretty soon we were able to take off our furs and begin drying them on wood rods that cross the inside of the structure at regular intervals. Tugged on the poles and found them very strong, as is the entire structure.

My feet seem fine — the numbness began to go away after a half hour baking near the fire. Now they tingle painfully, which I prefer to not having any feeling in them at all. York is still kneading his toes between his fingers to get feeling back into them.

And now to have my supper of two crackers and a few chews of dried meat. Wonder how Mr. Lewis and Joe and the men at camp are doing? Wonder how the rest of the crew is doing? And the cat? Said something to York who looked up and said, "Don't worry about anyone but yourself," and then went back to rubbing his toes again. A second later, he added, "And the cat's probably been eaten already."

September 21

York woke me early in the a.m. by handing me a piece of leather and saying, "Here's breakfast." He was already chewing his and since he seemed serious, I began working mine between my teeth, too.

He told me this was to save as much real food as possible because he had no idea when he'd find a settlement. I mentioned that he'd forgotten I was a part of the search and he waved my objection aside. His plan was this: I would go back to the boat and bring the men here to the village, leaving a note behind for Mr. Lewis. York was going south alone to find civilization.

When I said the plan wouldn't work, York got angry until I reminded him that I couldn't get across the river alone and that even if I could Frenchie and Stephen would need his strong arms to get them across.

This quieted York down. He sat chewing on his piece of leather like a mad dog and glaring at the fire. After a while he admitted I was right and that he should go back for the others. "But don't go and get lost out there," he warned me, adding, "I don't want that Joe to be first back to the men with help, you hear?" And then he put on his boots and gloves and stalked out of the longhouse.

So I will chew on my leather a few minutes more and add wood to the fire so that there might be warm embers when the others reach here later tonight. Then I am off.

Later

Horrible day. The way along the coast got rockier and harder to travel, plus a miserable, cold rain began falling in the p.m. Thought many times of giving up and going back to the longhouse and its warm fire. But without food I would only be going back to starve. So on I went.

My gloves wore through after several hours of climbing. Hands scratched and numb. Keep going, I told myself. Sometimes I worked right along the edge of the cliff with the sea a hundred or two hundred feet below. Other times, I had to travel a half mile inland because the route was easier.

Light was fading when I made my way back to the coast and saw something in the mist I didn't believe. A half mile offshore a steamship was slowly making passage north. First, I screamed and waved my arms like a wild man to get its attention. That didn't work.

A fire was my second thought. Had four matches for my journey and I set about searching for something to burn — anything! Found some twigs and small sticks, mostly wet, then ripped a few pages from the back of this journal. Struck the first match, and in my excitement I shook the flame out!

The ship was nearly even with me by this time and I knew I had to get that fire lit fast. Struck a second match and cupped it in my hands as I lowered it to the paper. The paper caught fire and flared up, licking at the wood. I remember whispering to the wood to please burn.

Wood crackled and the flame grew a little bigger, then — I don't know why, the wetness of the wood, a puff of wind — the flame wavered and died. I cussed my bad luck out loud, then spun around and started screaming and jumping about again. I was angry at myself for fumbling with the fire, angry at the wind, angry at the men on the ship for not being alert enough to see me.

I could have tried another match, but that would have left me just one and the ship was already past me and gliding along on its journey north. Could not even run after it because the ground was so uneven and rough in all directions.

So I watched the ship until it disappeared into the mist, which was when I let out a powerful sigh. Maybe York and those at the boat will be able to attract the boat's fool attention.

I went on then, bringing along my sorry collection of twigs and sticks and gathering up any others I came across as I made my way around and over the rocks. This is a d——nable place, not fit for man nor beasts nor even decent trees. Would give anything to be back in San Francisco town with Sean Michael.

Found a small hollow where I deposited my sorry collection of wood and soon had a tiny fire going, using both matches to accomplish this. It will not last much longer and my matches are now gone. Tomorrow will be a very cold day.

September 22

Cannot believe my fingers are warm enough to hold this pencil and that I am dry at last. And safe. I would have never guessed this would happen when I opened my eyes this a.m. to find snow and an icy rain coming down. I could hardly unbend my fingers or stand up I was so numb with the cold. As I started walking south, I remember thinking my luck couldn't get any worse. But it did anyway.

Went over some very steep ledges and around some very rugged, nasty hills. I probably traveled two miles *around* hills for every half mile *down* the coast. Stopped at noon and devoured — earned my nickname again! — the last of my food.

Gave myself a real talking to in order to continue in the p.m. Keep moving, I told myself, if you intend to save your shipmates. If you ever want to see Sean Michael again. The only good thing about this snowy day was that I could scoop up snow and let it melt in my mouth.

Which is what I was doing while leaping from one rock to another when I slipped and fell. My knee crashed against a sharp edge and I tumbled to the ground hard enough to knock all of the wind out of me.

What a poor wretch I was then, lying on the cold ground and thinking that I was all alone in the world and that if I died no one would ever find my body here among this mess of rocks. Like one of those frozen sailors Watty told us about. Thought fondly of Sean Michael and home — where the stove would be warm and where I could toast a thick piece of bread and smear it with the sweet orange jelly Pa likes.

I closed my eyes to better picture the scene. Could smell the toast, it was so real. I admit that I could have dreamt about this delicious treat all the p.m. In fact, I was nodding off with this pleasant vision in my head when I remembered the men back at our boat and York's warning not to fail. And Sean Michael. I couldn't quit and leave him alone and wondering why I had disappeared.

Then this other voice in my head said it was okay to take a little nap. Five or ten minutes out of a whole day isn't so much time to rest, the voice whispered. And I *was* tired. Watty would have said I had all of the gimp taken out of me I was so exhausted.

The next second Watty's face swam before my eyes. Then the faces of the rest of the crew. Then Sean Michael was there, too. It was like a picture of a family — everybody staring at me, depending on me.

I can tell you I was annoyed that such thoughts had squeezed out my wonderful toast and jelly. Another voice floated through my head saying that Mr. Lewis would be disappointed if I just gave up. That I would be disappointed with myself.

My eyes popped open. And so did my mouth as I said over and over again, "Get up, get up, get up right now!" I was on my feet, over that rock, and moving south again a few moments later.

Cannot say I traveled very fast after this. I was all done in and my legs were weak and heavy. But I kept on as best I could. And when I stopped to rest I never sat down because I worried that the bread and jelly picture would reappear in my head to tempt me. Instead, I stood still a minute or two, then — to get myself going again — I would jump up and down and scream as loud as I could.

If you do this four or five times during a journey you will begin to feel very silly, as I did. Once after doing my little act, I glanced at my gloves, fur pants, and canvas-covered feet and laughed out loud. Every inch of clothing was not only wet, but dirty and shredded by all of my rock climbing. Sean Michael would think I was a crazy man if he passed me on the street.

I wasn't much afraid after this. Just continued throughout the p.m. making slow progress south. Sometimes my route took me so close to the edge that I could hear the water slapping at the rocks below me. But when darkness began to fall, I did begin to fret. Knew I couldn't travel at night and would have to find a comfortable bunch of rocks to settle in. And without a fire, I wondered if I might fall asleep and never wake up again.

I had stopped while I thought about this. The ground nearby was littered with rocks and I knew I needed to find a better place to lay down my weary body. So I went into my act again, jumping all around and singing out a rhyme I'd made to cheer me up: "Hey, ho, rum will make you pink/Throw our stupid captain in the icy drink!" And I didn't mean a drink of rum, either.

A second later a terrible frenzy of growling and

snarling erupted not many feet away. Wolves, I thought, and I will soon be their dinner. I turned to get away, thinking I had to be the most unlucky boy in the entire world, when I heard something else — a string of the most creative cusses I'd ever heard. Better even than Little Joe can concoct!

It turned out to be a man's voice and he was yelling at the noisy creatures to shut up. The thought "They are dogs" popped into my head, followed by "I am saved!!!"

Went in the direction of the barking and there was a man standing at the door to his cabin trying to quiet his team of sled dogs. Who started in growling and snarling and barking and straining on their leads to get at me the moment they spotted me. The man saw me and said, "How the h——l did you get here?"

That was a good enough greeting for me — certainly more pleasant than many I received on the *Florence*. I went down to his cabin — carefully going wide of the snapping dogs. It was then I noticed there were four other sturdy-looking cabins just beyond this first one, each windowless but with friendly trails of smoke coming from their stovepipes.

He got me inside and in front of his stove, peppering me with questions the whole time. Who was I? What ship? What happened? On and on and on. I answered as best as I could, though I was shivering and my words came out as jagged as any of the rocks I'd gone over.

He was an English-speaking Norwegian named Anderson and I'd happened upon the whaling station at Cape Lisburne. Asked if he could help me get food and clothes to my friends, but he was too astonished by the route I'd taken — or more to the point, by the fact that I'd made it in one piece. When I asked again for help, he said, "You are in luck there, son. Supply steamer has arrived today and is anchored out there. She can go for them tomorrow first sun."

I relaxed then for the first time in days. Anderson then went off to fetch some of his neighbors, saying they would love to meet the man sturdy and foolish enough to go wandering down along the coast. That tiny cabin was soon crowded with folk — Anderson's neighbors, plus the first mate and Captain of the steamer. Turned out to be the *General Grant*, the same that led us up through the ice some weeks before.

Anderson brought out some spirits, but I refused to drink, saying I would wait until my friends could join me. Really, I did not want to put any rum in my very empty stomach for fear of what it might do to my thinking.

One of Anderson's neighbors, Tom Steele, had brought along a skillet of caribou steaks that must have tasted very good because I gobbled down one and asked for more. When the men laughed at my appetite, I told them how I'd gotten my nickname and they all agreed I was well and properly named.

Later

Tom Steele and Captain Bonam of the *General Grant* have charts of the coast and they are planning the rescue of the men at the Esquimaux village and those on the *Florence*. Anderson said that if we landed where he thinks we did, then Mr. Lewis and Joe will be at the village, too. Seems there is a river one day north of our landing place that is too wide and too fast-moving to cross and takes many days inland travel to find a crossable area. So it really is important that I found this supply station.

I must have looked all done in because Anderson suddenly announced that it was time to get some rest. Steele and the Captain left and Anderson showed me to my bed. My bed. Not some wood slats with a thin mattress of straw. A real bed with a soft mattress and thick blanket. I am going to finish this up and then pull those covers over my head and if I am lucky I will not wake up for several days.

September 23

Anderson woke me at first light and after a hasty cup of coffee — that tasted like real coffee beans were used to brew it! — Captain Bonam, Tom Steele, and I were brought aboard the *General Grant*. Even though the throb and clank of this steamer is strange to me, it feels good to have a ship swaying under my feet as it plunges through the water.

Steele is a guide and knows the countryside like a farmer knows his pasture. He has stationed himself on deck and is scanning the shoreline for any signs of life. In addition, the Captain blows the steam horn every fifteen minutes to alert those on shore. Not long after we left, Steele pointed toward the rocky cliffs and said to me, "That is a nasty tumble of rocks you crossed. The worst in this whole territory."

He was right. The rocks rose up a hundred feet and more from the water, some sharp and dangerous-looking, others deceptively smooth and slick with ice. Here and there, the trail even appeared — the trail I'd stumbled over yesterday. If I'd slipped the wrong way, I realized, I'd have gone bouncing down the cliff and into the cold water. Good thing I was so numb and desperate or I might have understood the danger and given up.

It will take the better part of the day to reach the Esquimaux camp, according to Steele. I spend most of my time belowdecks with the mates, either reading their collection of old newspapers or writing in this journal. Did get a tour of the engine room — a tiny space crowded with pipes and steam and a boiler that roars constantly for more coal, while two giant pistons — that's what the boiler chief called them — move back and forth to turn the propeller shaft. I can imagine what Little Joe would say about this hot, metal monster and I have to admit that I much prefer the quiet running of our sails to this racket.

Later when I was on deck Captain Bonam told me that after picking up Mr. Lewis and the others, he'll search for the men on the ice, then head north to Point Barrow to deliver supplies. Then, if the ice hasn't blocked him, he'll be going south to San Francisco town. He will be taking the sick and injured back with him, and he wanted to know if I want to go, too.

I hesitated and said I wasn't sure. "Don't worry about that captain of yours," Captain Bonam told me. "He was a d——d fool to get lost in the ice and worse for risking his crew by going back to the ship." But it wasn't the Captain I was thinking of. It was the crew — especially those waiting at the Esquimaux village — and Mr. Lewis. I do not want to let any of them down by leaving them behind, especially if Captain Blaine decides to press charges.

Felt guilty immediately when I thought this. I left Sean Michael behind because I thought it would help him and Pa. But I won't know if I was right in this unless I go back to see for myself. If it was, then fine. But if Pa is still his drunk, angry self, then I have to get Sean Michael out of there somehow.

Decided finally to talk with Mr. Lewis. If he says it is okay to go back, then I will. If not, I will stay until my time is up here and then go south to San Francisco town.

Am going on deck to stand watch with Steele.

Late p.m.

Ice had drifted away from the cliffs so our passage north went smoothly, but the clouds grew dark and heavy as the hours crept by. Steele thought it might begin snowing and worried that this could delay the rescue for a day or more. I was just beginning to lose hope when I noticed a change in the way the clouds looked some two miles away.

Felt a tingle inside — like that first time I spotted a whale spouting in the great wide sea. Studied the thin vapor closely to be sure. Then I pointed and said to Steele, "There! Do you see it? Smoke."

He didn't at first, but then he squinted hard and shielded his eyes from the snow's glare and gave out a smile. Captain Bonam was informed and he ordered that the ship's little cannon — which they carry to signal other ships in fog and snow — be charged and fired. This was carried out and very soon a person appeared on the cliff and immediately commenced jumping and leaping about. Two others joined him and I have to tell you the three did a lively dance up there.

It took a while to get the *General Grant* to where the men were, anchor it, and then get a boat ashore. Little Joe and York had come down the rock face to meet us and Little Joe shouted, "What took you so long, Wolf? My crippled old grandma coulda walked to San Fran and back in the time it took you!" York told him to show more respect for "our wanderin' boy" — though his language was much saltier than that — and then Little Joe said he was only joking.

As predicted by Tom Steele, Mr. Lewis and Joe had failed to find a place to cross the wide river and had come back to join the others. Stephen's cough is still with him and a fever has set in as well. He is finally as sick as he looks. Frenchie was hobbling about on a pair of crudely constructed crutches complaining that the longhouse was too warm and that he felt closed in. Funny he never complained that the forecastle was too hot or cramped.

Captain Bonam wanted us to be aboard the *General*

Grant before the light was gone so we could steam off in search of Captain Blaine and the other men as early as possible. So we are aboard the *General Grant* now. The sick men are in the Captain's cabin. Mr. Lewis is bunking with the ship's first mate, while the rest of us have taken up positions in the mess room. I fit very snugly under the plank table with a burlap bag of dried peas for a pillow.

And here is a confession. I did not ask Mr. Lewis about going south with Captain Bonam. I could have, but I didn't. Tom Steele told everyone that I'd traveled over land that many experienced trappers and even the Esquimaux fear and everyone clapped me on the back and said I'd done well. Later, Mr. Lewis came over to tell me he was proud of the way I'd handled myself. Could have asked then, but I hesitated — I think because I did not want to disappoint Mr. Lewis by saying I wanted to be away from him. And yet there is still Sean Michael and my father to worry over.

September 29

It was snowing by the time light appeared on the 24th. Snow was fairly heavy, but Captain Bonam said we could not wait because the wind might come up and drive the ice farther to the west. He talked with Mr. Lewis about the last known location of the *Florence*, then we steamed north up the coast. Captain Bonam stayed in open water near the coast for several hours, before turning his ship into the ice and toward the *Florence*. Or at least toward where we thought she was.

The ice was easy to slice through at first, and even when the pieces grew thicker the *General Grant*'s iron hull chopped them in half and pushed them aside. Little Joe was impressed with how the steamship handled the ice, but he still added, "Give me warm weather and a sailing ship any time."

Late in the second day of the search, Captain Bonam ordered the ship stopped because the ice was growing too thick. A party was put together to go out on the ice with Tom Steele in charge. Mr. Lewis told me I would stay on the *General Grant*, saying "You need to let some others have a chance at being the hero, Wolf." And so Mr. Lewis, Little Joe, Joe, York, and Steele set off, along with two crew members of the *General Grant*.

I did not see how they could find the crew of the *Florence* in the endless ice. Watty set in telling us tales about miraculous rescues in the Arctic — men lost for days and weeks in the worst weather who were spotted miles off, etc. I might have taken some comfort in these except that Captain Bonam kept pacing his ship with a very worried look to him. The only cheering thing was that late on the second day the snow stopped and the sky began to clear.

In the p.m. of the third day, I was on deck searching the horizon when I began to hear a distant rumbling. Must have looked puzzled because the Captain came over and said the ice a mile or more off was beginning to move, probably because of some storm far to the north.

This set me to fretting even more. Then just before the light disappeared, Watty sang out, "Thar! Movement on the ice!" Searched the distant horizon and saw one tiny dot, then another, and another. They were a half day's march away. But they were there and safe.

Captain Bonam had lights hung in the rigging to guide the men and by dawn the next morning the first of the men began to arrive, guided by Tom Steele. Others trooped in throughout the a.m. — which meant a number of celebrations during the day as more and more men crowded belowdecks to find a warm spot to rest and tell us their story.

It seems that on the march back to the *Florence* John Kenealy wandered from the rest to pee and fell through the ice. The fog was so thick at the time that it took a while before anyone could locate where he'd gone in and by then it was too late. He'd been swallowed up and that was the end of him.

The mood among the crew worsened when they

finally reached the *Florence*. The lower holds where the oil and bone were stored had flooded, but the forecastle and officers' cabins were still pretty much intact. And even though a wiggle of the ice might suddenly send the entire ship to the bottom, Captain Blaine ordered that they stay the night.

The men — officers and crew alike — refused to remain, at which point the Captain drew his pistol and even fired a shot into the air to stop their going. He even seized the cask containing the ambergris and said only those who obeyed him would receive money from its sale. Heated words followed — I can't imagine what some of them were! — but in the end the men turned and left the ship and Captain behind.

Almost six hours after the last of the forecastle hands appeared, Captain Blaine finally straggled in, alone and miserable looking. When it was learned that somewhere during the night he'd abandoned the ambergris, there was a rush of angry words and threats. Captain Bonam soon quieted the men and then he put Captain Blaine in a small storage space, where he remains hidden away and safe. And so our oil, bone, and ambergris — our hard work — have all been lost to the ice.

Captain Bonam did not like the look of the sky and had the *General Grant* heading toward Point Barrow as quickly as possible. He was worried that a storm might trap him up here for days, if not the entire winter. When I heard that I went immediately to Mr. Lewis and asked if I could go south on the *General Grant* and told him why I wanted to leave.

Mr. Lewis looked surprised by my request and I thought for a moment that he would say no. But then he smiled and said, "If anyone deserves to leave here it's you, Wolf."

I was relieved to hear this and even happier when he added, "But I hope you don't turn your back on the sea. You have a gift for navigating and move about a ship with ease."

Word got around quickly that I would be leaving, and Frenchie, York, and Watty came over to congratulate me. "An' don't ferget yer friends," Watty said more loudly than necessary, "when yer havin' a meal of real honest-to-goodness un-spoilt food." Cookie of course overheard his remark, which set him off sputtering and defending his cooking. Pretty soon the entire crew joined in the fun.

The only unpleasant moment came when I passed Ethan and he muttered, "and good riddance." Stopped and thought to confront him, but then changed my mind. In a few days I will be heading south, while he will be stuck up here for months. So I just smiled and said, "Enjoy the snow, Ethan."

Since then I have been thinking of my time on the *Florence*. We left San Francisco town and traveled 2,000 miles to Honolulu, then another 4,500 miles to wind up here. Along the way I have made a few fast friends who I do not want to forget. Even feel close to Nathaniel — despite his eternal praying. I've also had my share of adventures and only a few of them have been bad.

And it is Sean Michael I want to share my tales with. As for Pa, he is who he is, especially when he drinks, and I don't have to like that or take it, either. And maybe living with the likes of York and Ethan has made me more tolerant of my father's ways. Only time will tell. Besides, all of my climbing in the rigging and over the rocks has added muscle to my frame and Pa will probably think twice before he does anything.

So I will spend my next few days packing my few possessions and thinking of home. Funny that I used that word. Home. When I fled it I tried to banish it from my head — I guess to make my escape easier on myself. But it would not let me off that easily and I must say I am very happy it did not.

EPILOGUE

Captain Blaine never brought charges against any of his crew and was eventually fired by the whaling company for incompetence. The healthy men wintered in Point Barrow and found places on the whalers that docked there in the spring. Eventually, a new steam whaler was built to replace the *Florence* and Mr. Lewis was made Captain.

Wolf reached home in late October and was greeted warmly by both Sean Michael and their father. He stayed with them for three weeks and spent many evenings reading sections of his journal to his brother. His father sat in on these readings and one night he blurted out, "Why, that is a cracking good tale, son."

His father still drank too much, but he had changed over the months that Wolf was gone. He still complained about his boss, still complained about the housework or how a meal had been prepared, but he did not bear down on Wolf quite so hard. Sean Michael did not think it had to do with his brother's newly developed muscles, though

Wolf had grown enough that he did not fit into any of his old clothes. Their father had lost a wife and then he thought he'd lost a son, Sean Michael reasoned, so he knew that a harsh word or a slap might very well send one *or both* of his sons away forever. Even so, Wolf was never completely at ease with his father, though nights watching the stars from the roof did help.

Wolf did return to the sea, but not on a whaler. He remembered so clearly the look in the harpooned whale's eye as it swam past that he could not see himself killing another. So he signed on as an able seaman aboard a steam freighter taking goods from San Francisco to Japan.

Over the years he went from able seaman, to mate, and was finally made Captain of his own ship when he was just twenty-four years old. He continued crossing the Pacific for another forty-two years, visiting his family and friends whenever possible. He married a girl from his neighborhood when he was twenty-six, and they had six children.

He often inquired after his friends from the *Florence*, and was able to learn something of what happened to them over the years. Frenchie and Watty left the north as soon as they could and signed on whalers operating in the warm waters off Australia. York and most of the other men remained in the north to whale for as long as work was available. One of the few crewmembers Wolf actually met again was Ethan, who happened to be in Japan at the same time Wolf was some ten years after their cruise. Ethan greeted Wolf as if he was his best friend and during a long chat never once mentioned the bad blood that had existed between them. So Watty was right after all, Wolf told himself afterward. Ethan's anger finally ran out of steam.

Wolf received several letters from Nathaniel, who had stayed in the Alaskan territory to teach and preach to the native people. In one of Nathaniel's letters he thanked Wolf for all of the help he had given him onboard the *Florence*, but did not say a thing about those times Wolf had barked at him. He ended each letter with a quote from the Bible, for which Nathaniel always apologized in advance.

Wolf kept one of these letters tucked inside his journal, which he brought along without fail on his many voyages. Often, when on deck at night, his ship gently rocking, he would study the vast sky and stars and recall the closing lines: "Be watchful, stand firm in your faith, be courageous, be strong. Let all that you do be done in love."

LIFE IN AMERICA
IN *1874*

HISTORICAL NOTE

The history of the United States is joined intimately with the history of the whaling industry. In 1602, a book published in England to lure prospective colonists to the New World promised that "whales of the best kind for oil and bone [baleen] are said to abound near Cape Cod. . . ." And when the Pilgrims entered Plymouth Bay in 1620, one crew member recalled that they were greeted by whales "playing hard by the *Mayflower*, [and that] many of [the passengers] were eager to undertake their pursuit. . . ."

Because whales were plentiful and swam close to the shore, many towns, such as Salem, Nantucket, and Cape Cod, began sending out ships to hunt them. The first whales taken were usually right whales: They were the "right" whale to hunt because they were slow swimmers, floated when dead, and provided huge quantities of oil and baleen. A sixty-foot-long right whale might have anywhere from 48,000 to 64,000 pounds of blubber, while its mouth contained approximately 540 long baleen plates.

In addition to providing fuel for lamps, the oil cooked out of the blubber was made into candles, soap, and a variety of other cosmetics; it was also valued as a lubricant for all sorts of machinery (from large, factory steam engines to sewing machines). The baleen were very flexible and could be fashioned into a number of useful objects, including corset stays, combs, buggy whips, and springs.

The need for whale oil and baleen increased as manufacturing expanded in the nineteenth century. To keep up with demand, whaling fleets grew in number until more than 750 ships were going out every year and thousands of whales were killed and processed.

One immediate result of this massive hunting was the disappearance of right whales along the Atlantic coast. The idea that overhunting might be driving local whale herds toward extinction was not understood in the nineteenth century; whalers believed that the whales had simply been frightened away to other parts of the world's oceans. So whaling ships began to venture farther and farther out to sea to hunt. Other kinds of whales were taken, including another species of massive baleen whale, the bowhead, and the much more aggressive sperm whale (which did not have baleen, but yielded an extraordinarily high grade of oil). Eventually, whaling ships from the United States would sail all the way around the southern tip of South America and into the Pacific Ocean in search of their valuable prey.

These voyages covered thousands of miles and could take anywhere from two to four years to complete, though sometimes it took even longer to fill the hold. One ship, the *Nile*, left New London, Connecticut, in May 1858 and did not return to port until April 1869 — a voyage of eleven years! Most family men did not want to be away from home for such extended periods of time, so companies were forced to look elsewhere for their crews — criminals, drunks, those unfamiliar with whaling or sailing ships, and even boys.

Every ship brought along one or two cabin boys, who might be as young as ten years old. A cabin boy's job was to help prepare and serve meals, clean the officers' living quarters, refill the oil lamps, and do other small chores. But if a regular seaman became ill or died (events that were all too common on a whaler), the cabin boy often took over that man's duties as well. And while mid-nineteenth-century laws stipulated that parental permission was needed before a boy under the age of seventeen could work on a whaler as a regular crewmember, it wasn't very difficult for a tall and determined fourteen- or fifteen-year-old to sign papers.

No one knows how many underage boys went to sea, because a ship's records were usually very vague in nature. But in the instances where detailed records were kept, an analysis reveals that one-third of the twenty-six common seamen were teenagers. It's clear that thousands upon thousands of boys joined in this dangerous and deadly work, and a surprising number of them left behind diaries and journals about their experiences.

These written records tell us that they signed on for many reasons. Some were trying to escape an abusive parent or to earn money to help their families. George Fred Tilton stowed away aboard a whaler because he was envious of a friend who had already gone to sea. Many others left home simply because they wanted to get away from boring farm chores and see distant, exotic lands. What they found was mostly hard and often brutal work.

No one who stepped aboard a whaler was ever coddled. It cost too much money to build a ship and outfit it for an extended voyage to allow any sort of slacking. Besides, everyone aboard — from the Captain down to the cabin boy — participated in the profits of a voyage. Maximum profits were made through consistently hard work. Sailors — even the boys — understood this and would not tolerate laziness or sloppy work because they knew it would come out of their pockets.

The drive to maintain a healthy margin of profit fostered many innovations in the way whales were hunted. The harpoon gun was perfected in 1864 by a Norwegian named Svend Foyn, and the steam chaser capable of speeds of more than fifteen knots appeared in 1875. The latter was particularly important because it allowed seamen to go after even the fastest whales, including the sie, minke, fin, and the largest mammal on earth: the 100-foot-long, 150,000-ton blue whale.

Once steam chasers replaced the old sailing ships, no ocean was left unhunted, and no whale was safe. In the early twentieth century, factory ships from many countries made their appearance, and the killing of whales escalated. In this system of hunting, small and speedy boats are used to kill the whales. Other small boats drag the carcass back to giant ships where they are hauled aboard, cut up, and processed, and the oil is stored. In 1913, more than 25,000 whales were killed; by 1938, nearly 55,000 were taken. Blue whales were hunted to near extinction, as their population in the southern hemisphere went from 225,000 at the beginning of the twentieth century to between only 200 and 400 animals in the early 1960s.

By this time, the United States was completely out of the whaling business. Petroleum, plastic, and light, springy metals had replaced the more expensive oil and baleen. In addition, environmental groups were finally beginning to convince people in our country and around the world that the extinction of many kinds of whales was at hand. Once the world's greatest killer of whales, the United States soon became one of their greatest defenders.

Even countries that wanted to continue to hunt whales, such as Japan, the Soviet Union, Norway, and Iceland, eventually began to see reality. Despite year-round hunting and a highly efficient factory ship system, they simply couldn't find enough whales to make their businesses profitable. In 1982, the International Whaling Commission, a worldwide organization comprised of more than one hundred whaling countries, officially banned the hunting of all whales.

Some countries still insist on sending out ships to hunt whales, but the number killed each year has dropped to less than 1,000 at this time. This reduced hunting has allowed whale populations to slowly climb again. And with this, a different sort of "hunting" has developed: whale watching. The new whaling fleet of the United States has more than 400 craft leaving from 200 locations on the east and west coast, plus Alaska and Hawaii. Almost four million people take to the sea every year to watch these giants of the ocean swim, frolic, and breach the water in magnificent displays of grace and power.

The whaling ship Sea Breeze *heads out of San Francisco Bay, toward Alaskan waters, in 1890.*

The deck of an Arctic whaling ship is filled with sailors hard at work, as well as livestock and dogs.

Whaling ships are stuck on the Arctic ice as crewmen walk on the icebergs and row out in smaller boats to hunt whales.

The enormous polar right whale is beached on a shelf of ice.

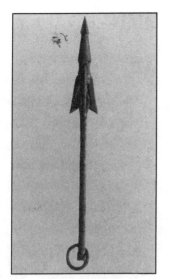
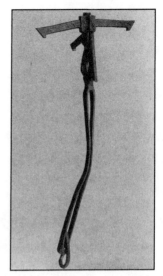

When a whaler thrusts a harpoon at a whale, it is closed and arrowlike, but once it pierces the whale's skin, it opens, as pictured on the right.

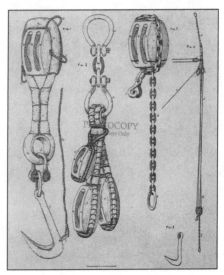

Some of the types of cutting tackle used for butchering a whale.

Having caught a whale, sailors on a whaling ship keep it alongside the boat as they pull its skin off in strips.

Long pieces of baleen were cleaned and bundled before being sent to market where they could fetch as much as seven dollars a pound.

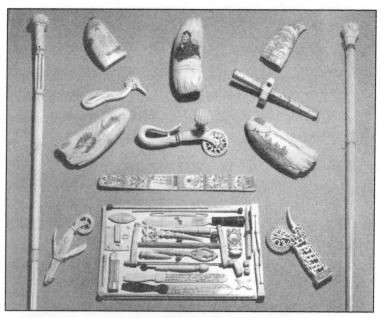

Whale products were used to make all sorts of ornamental and functional items, such as ladies' corsets, doctor's tools, canes, and scrimshaw — teeth and rib bones painted and etched by sailors during long journeys.

About the Author

"I became interested in whales after encountering a number of minke and humpback whales off the coast of Provincetown, Massachusetts, during a whale-watching voyage. One of the humpbacks — a forty-five-ton female, according to the naturalist aboard the *Dolphin VII* — actually rose up out of the water at the side of our ship and used her powerful tail flukes to "stand" there, not more than ten feet from me. For several unbelievable moments we were eye to eye, and then she gently edged away from the ship and sank back into the water. Trust me, this is the kind of encounter you never forget, and it sent me off to the library to learn more about these giants of the sea and how we humans have treated them over the past centuries."

Jim Murphy is the author of more than thirty books for children, including *The Great Fire*, which was named a Newbery Honor Book; *Blizzard!*, which was named a Sibert Award Honor Book; and for the Dear America series, *West to a Land of Plenty: The Diary of Teresa Angelino Viscardi* and *My Face to the Wind: The Diary of Sarah Jane Price, a Prairie Teacher*. For the My Name Is America series, he wrote *The Journal of James Edmond Pease, a Civil War Union Soldier*.

FOR MY EDITORS
TRACY MACK AND BETH S. LEVINE—
WHOSE INTELLIGENT COMMENTS AND SUGGESTIONS
(AND OCCASIONAL PRODDING)
HELPED ME GET BRIAN'S VOYAGE ONTO PAPER.

ACKNOWLEDGMENTS

Grateful acknowledgment is made for permission to reprint the following:

Cover Portrait: The National Maritime Museum, San Francisco, courtesy of the Melville Library, South Street Seaport Museum, New York.

Cover Background: The Granger Collection, New York.

Page 180 (top): Whaling ship, Culver Pictures, New York.

Page 180 (bottom): Deck of a whaling ship, University of Alaska Archives, no. 66-10-117, Fairbanks, Alaska.

Page 181 (top): Whaling ships cut through Arctic ice, *Hull Whalers in the Arctic* by Thomas A. Binks, courtesy of the Ferens Art Gallery, Hull City Museums and Art Galleries, UK/ Bridgeman Art Library, New York.

Page 181 (bottom): Right whale on the ice, The Granger Collection, New York.

Page 182 (top): Harpoons, Brown Brothers, New York.

Page 182 (bottom): Cutting tools, North Wind Picture Archives, Alfred, Maine.

Page 183 (top): Whale being butchered, Culver Pictures, New York.

Page 183 (bottom): Selling whalebone, Nantucket Historical Association, from the Stackpole Collection, Nantucket, Massachusetts.

Page 184 (top): Items made from whalebone, Nantucket Historical Association, from the Stackpole Collection, Nantucket, Massachusetts.

Page 184 (bottom): Ladies' corsets, The Granger Collection, New York.

While the events described and some of the characters in this book may be based on actual historical events and real people, Brian Doyle is a fictional character, created by the author, and his journal and its epilogue are works of fiction.

Library of Congress Cataloging-in-Publication Data

Murphy, Jim, 1947–
The Journal of Brian Doyle: a Greenhorn on an Alaskan Whaling Ship /
by Jim Murphy.
p. cm. — (My Name Is America)
Summary: In 1874, Brian Doyle records in his diary how he ran away from
his home in San Francisco, joined the crew of a whaling ship, and endured
storms, hostile shipmates, and being stranded in the Arctic.
ISBN 0-439-07814-8
[1. Whaling — Fiction.   2. Ocean voyages — Fiction.
3. Survival — Fiction.   4. Diaries — Fiction.]
I. Title.   II. Series.
PZ7.M9535 Jv 2003
[Fic] 21   2002044578
CIP   AC

10 9 8 7 6 5 4 3 2 1   04 05 06 07 08

The display type was set in Pelican
The text type was set in Berling Roman
Book design by Elizabeth B. Parisi
Photo research by Amla Sanghvi

Printed in the U.S.A.   23
First edition, April 2004